LOVE ON THE LINE

A Christian Football Romance

LORANA HOOPES

To my wonderful readers who inspire me to write everyday.
To my father who got me into watching football when I was
young.
To Emmitt Smith who was my favorite ball player of all
time. He had so much class, and I loved how he finished
his degree as well. Such an inspiration!

BLAINE

Blaine watched as his friend and teammate Tucker Jackson dropped to one knee, but his eyes weren't on the happy couple. Instead, they were drawn to the stunning brunette who stood behind them holding the mic out for the proposal to be heard while trying her best to blend into the background so as not to be a distraction. As if that was possible for her. With her dark velvet locks pulled up on top of her head, the slender curve of her neck was even more pronounced. Her skin glowed like fresh cream, and his eyes followed the lines of her neck to her slim shoulders before he shook his head to clear it.

He wondered how her skin might feel under his fingertips, but he had no business thinking about Kenzi like that. Not with Heidi, or was it Jennifer, he was seeing this week? It didn't matter. While Kenzi wasn't like the women he usually dated, she was too good for him. Besides, she deserved a man who could give her a future like Tucker was doing for Shelby, and that certainly wasn't him. He shouldn't even be thinking about settling down. Not with his past.

Still, since the day he'd met Kenzi, she'd made appearances in his mind. Not every day but often enough that he'd memorized the slight tilt of her upper lip, the way her eyes sparkled when she smiled. Enough to know that he thought of her more often than he should.

Cheering erupted around him, and he realized Shelby had said yes. She held her hand up for the crowd to see, and a tightness seized his heart. He wanted that - what Tucker had. He wanted a beautiful woman who would smile at him the way Shelby was smiling at Tucker now. Someone who would look at him with pride and admiration. A woman he could pamper and love and protect - but there was the rub. He wasn't good at protecting. He was great at pretending he was. Sometimes he even convinced himself he could do it. He was, after all, older now and wiser.

Maybe. But what if he failed again?

He knew he shouldn't - it was wrong, it was dangerous, it would never work - but as if they had a mind of their own, his feet pushed into the floor and he stood, clapping with those around him. Then he moved. Not towards the door where he should have been moving. Of course not to where he should be going. Fresh air. That's what he really needed. That would clear his head and push this stupid idea away, but then why were his feet moving away from the door? Away from the door and toward Kenzi. *Turn back*, he thought. But his feet did not seem to be getting the same message his brain was sending. Before he knew it, he stood before her.

"Hey, Blaine, I'm so glad you could come tonight." Her eyes sparkled like emeralds held under a light, and the sincerity of her smile only deepened her beauty. Oh man, was he in trouble.

"Thanks. You did an amazing job with the place." He'd volunteered a few times since the Christmas party last year, but he was still in awe of how many improvements Kenzi had managed to do to the bland building in such a short time.

Her gaze scanned around the room, and he could see the pride on her face. "Thanks. There was more that I wanted to do, but we couldn't keep using the church forever. The kids need this space." Her eyes came back to his, and the corners or her mouth lifted in another smile - one that made his heart do funny things inside his chest. "I hear you'll be volunteering around here more often."

"I will. Each of us will be hosting a day a month, but I figured I would set an example and do more than that. My hope is that more of the players will follow. You and Shelby have certainly done something amazing here."

She shook her head, sending the dark tendrils that framed her face bouncing. How he wanted to touch those tendrils, to see if they felt as soft as they looked. "Shelby is the one who has done amazing work. I simply did what she needed. Working at the center was never my dream, but I'm glad I was able to help her fulfill hers."

"And decorating? Is that your dream?" Blaine had been following the scuttlebutt he could gather from Shelby and Tucker, and he knew that Kenzi was finishing her certificate in interior design.

Her lips pursed in an adorable position as her head tilted slightly. "I think so. I'm really enjoying school and doing this was so much fun."

"Do you think you'd be open to doing a cabin?" He broke out in a sweat. He could feel it along his hairline. What was he doing? Inviting her into that house - even though it didn't feel like his house - was dangerous, but he couldn't seem to stop himself. There was something about Kenzi that made him want to put his guard down and figure himself out so he could have nice things. One side of him knew it was impossible to ever not feel this heavy burden of guilt; that was the cold sweat part. The other half wanted more than anything to try and be better; that was the mouth part.

Her head cocked a little farther to the right as her eyes

narrowed at him. "Are you looking for a designer, Blaine Hollis?"

His name sounded like honey from her lips, and he forced himself to remain aloof even though the way she looked into his eyes like that terrified him. Could she see his demons? "Maybe. If you're up to it, but it's probably a lost cause, I don't know." He stumbled, trying to backtrack and maneuver away from his betraying mouth. "I've inherited a lakeside cabin, but I don't know what to do with it. I'm probably just going to sell it." He should have sold it already with all the ghosts it held, all the memories, but some of them were good memories. "I've looked at a few designers but haven't found any I liked and trusted. Until now."

As if gauging his sincerity, her eyes searched his face. "I'd be happy to come take a look, but it would be my first real job. I mean this was a job, but," she shrugged, "it's not the same as redecorating a house or cabin. I'd love to take a look and see if it's something I could do. I've been looking for things to add to my portfolio. Are you sure you want me?"

Was he sure he wanted her? If she only knew how loaded her words were. He wanted her more than he'd wanted a woman in a long time. "Yeah," he paused, feeling a lightness he hadn't felt since the last good day at the lake house. "I think I'm sure."

She walked over to a small table and picked up a

handbag before returning to him. His eyes followed her brightly painted nails as she flicked the clasp open and reached inside. A moment later, they reappeared with a pink business card and tilted towards him. "Here. Shelby got me some business cards as a graduation present. I don't know how she did pink, but I love it. It's so me. Anyway, my number's on here. Call me tomorrow and we'll set up a time to check it out, so I can see what I can do."

He took the pink business card from her and bit the inside of his lip. She couldn't do just a normal white business card like everyone else. Nope, she had to be different. The pink with gold sparkly letters fit her completely.

Blaine watched her walk away and then slipped the card into his pocket. He'd either just made the smartest move of his life or the dumbest. He just wasn't sure which.

KENZI

"Ooh, let me see." Kenzi squealed as she lifted Shelby's hand to critique the ring. She'd seen it earlier, of course, when Tucker had showed it to her before the proposal in order to make sure Shelby would like it, but diamonds always looked better on hands than in boxes - no matter how beautiful the velvet wrapping was. "It's perfect, Shelby. It's so you."

Shelby's eyes dropped to the ring and pure rays of

happiness shone from her gaze. "I know, right? It's just what I would have picked if I'd been asked. Did you help him pick it?"

Kenzi chuckled and shook her head. "Nope. He showed it to me after he had it just for reassurance you would love it, but picking it was all him."

Shelby's gaze wandered to her fiancé who was currently chatting and laughing with several other members of the team including Blaine Hollis and Mason Dixon. "I never thought I would find someone who knew me so well, and I certainly never expected him to be a football player."

"Yeah, I would never have believed it if someone had told me that either." Kenzi laughed and sat down in the chair next to her. Shelby had barely even known what football was before she met Tucker Jackson, much less how to play it, so it was completely ironic she was now engaged to a football player.

Shelby turned her gaze to Kenzi, a mischievous smile on her lips. "Now, we just need to find someone for you."

Kenzi held up her hands. "No, thanks, I'm good right now. Though Blaine Hollis did just offer me a job. I think. And he's a cutie. A little mysterious and intense, but a cutie."

Shelby's eyes lit up, and the mischievous smile was joined with a twinkling light. "A job, huh? Are you sure that wasn't code for a date?"

Kenzi shook her head. Her friend had jumped off the deep end. Shelby had always been a romantic, but put a ring on her finger and she was a regular Cupid shooting love arrows at anything that moved. "No, he wants me to redecorate some cabin he inherited." It definitely wasn't a date, because he would have actually asked her on a date if it was a date, right?

"Sure he does."

Shelby was on a roll tonight, but she might be able to give Kenzi some insight on Blaine, seeing as how she had spent more time with the team members. There were definitely some things Kenzi was curious about. "Do you know anything about the members of the Tornadoes? Blaine's been on the team for years and no one has ever seen him with the same girl more than once. Not once. Doesn't that seem odd to you?"

It certainly did to Kenzi. When she'd begun gaining interest in football about six years ago in order to impress a college quarterback, Blaine Hollis had been the first member of the Texas Tornadoes to catch her eye. With his blond hair and warm brown eyes, he exuded this odd mix of masculinity and sensitivity that Kenzi found attractive. She had figured she couldn't be the only one and had dug into his personal life, surprised when she found no mention of a steady girlfriend. Nor did they ever mention one on TV or show a woman in the stands. Occasionally he was spotted with a woman, but never the same woman twice.

Six years and still no relationship. He was either celibate or…

Shelby's voice interrupted her rabbit train of thought. "Maybe he just hasn't found the right woman yet."

"Maybe." Kenzi agreed because she knew there was no use arguing with Shelby when she was like this. She was sweet and loyal and stubborn as a mule when she wanted to be. Besides, it was possible she was right. Maybe Blaine was just waiting for the perfect woman, but Kenzi didn't think so.

2

SEVEN MONTHS EARLIER - BLAINE

Blaine Hollis paused, the weighted bar just inches from his chest, as the smart watch on his wrist vibrated, letting him know he was receiving a call. It was his workout time. Who in the world would be calling him right now? Everyone he was close friends with should be working out now too, and his family… well that was a whole other story. Surely nothing was wrong with them. He pushed the bar up and placed it back in the rack before glancing at his wrist. The unknown number only served to stir up the apprehension bubbling in his stomach.

He pulled his phone out of the arm band pouch, where it stayed nestled and sweat-free during his workout, and paused the Toby Mac song pumping through his ears before answering. "Hello?" The word came out labored due to the adrenaline coursing through his body.

"Blaine? It's Tucker. I need your help."

Tucker Jackson. Of course. If he'd checked his phone instead of his watch, he would have seen Tucker's name, but his watch only flashed numbers, and he had long ago stopped memorizing them. He should have guessed it was Tucker though. He was the only Texas Tornado team member not at workout practice right now because he'd been given emergency leave to return home due to his father's heart attack.

"Tucker? Aren't you supposed to be with your dad?" Blaine grabbed a towel from his bag and wiped it across his forehead.

"I am, and he's doing okay. I actually need help for the Christmas party tomorrow."

Blaine's hand froze. Had he missed a memo? He didn't remember hearing anything about a Christmas party. "What party, Tucker?"

"At the community center. I promised Shelby that I would bring presents for the kids."

"But aren't you in San Antonio?" Was Tucker asking him to bring presents to the center? He didn't have presents nor did he feel like going out and getting any, and somehow, he doubted Tucker had purchased any before leaving town.

He didn't mind kids, really, at least as long as they belonged to someone else and he only had to be around them for small windows of time. Anything longer than that dredged up memories that he wanted to keep hidden.

"I'm driving back tomorrow, so I can keep my word. Look, my sister Whitley is purchasing a ton of items and asking that they be available for collection at the stores in Southlake. Do you think you could round up a few guys to help you pick up the toys and help me deliver them tomorrow night?"

Blaine rolled his eyes, even though he knew Tucker couldn't see the gesture over the phone. Picking up toys was not how he had intended to spend his Christmas Eve, but it wasn't like he had much else planned. He certainly wasn't going home to a family. They hadn't spent a Christmas together in years, and bringing gifts to the kids at the center seemed like a worthy use of his time. "How many toys are we talking about?" He thought about his red Mustang - he wouldn't be putting many gifts in there.

"Fifty, at least."

"Fifty?" Blaine spat the word out in surprise. "I can't carry fifty toys in my car."

Tucker sighed on the other end. "Which is why I asked you to see if some of the guys could help out. Doesn't Mason have a large truck?"

Mason Dixon (his parents had an odd sense of humor) was one of the wide receivers on the team, and he did, indeed, drive a large, suped up truck. But Blaine didn't know if it would even hold fifty toys.

"Please, Blaine." The silence must have made Tucker think Blaine was refusing his request. "Those kids really deserve Christmas."

"Yeah, I get it. I was thinking of who else to ask." Though Blaine was not a fan of Christmas - not anymore anyway - he couldn't deny that the kids Tucker had been working with could probably use a little Christmas cheer. At least if the stories Tucker had told him were true. "Okay, I'll get it done. Where do you want to meet?"

"How about at the stadium? Can you gather a bunch of the guys?"

"I'll do my best, Tucker, but it is Christmas Eve we're talking about here. Some of the guys have little kids."

"Whatever you can manage, Blaine. Thanks. You're a lifesaver."

The phone went dead in his ear, and Blaine sighed. Not only had he lost a good five minutes of his workout, but he'd have to pause it a little longer to ask the guys about helping before they left for the day. It was a good thing no one would be waiting on him tonight because he had a late night ahead of him.

He found Mason and Rodney soaking in the hot tubs. They were a hot commodity after a hard workout. The two men must have already finished their workouts, and a small seed of jealousy stirred within him. A hot tub sounded so relaxing right about now. Well, at least Rodney drove a rather large truck as well. Maybe they would both agree and he could get back to his workout quickly.

"Hey guys, I have a favor to ask. Well, actually Tucker does."

Mason opened one eye and looked at Blaine. "Where is Tucker anyway?"

"Family emergency, but he's coming back tomorrow night. Evidently the center he's been volunteering at is having a Christmas party. He's asked that we collect the toys he ordered and bring them to the stadium tomorrow night. Can you guys help out?"

Rodney shrugged and nodded. "Sure. My family is local, so I can always visit them afterwards. What about you Mason?"

Mason's eyes shifted to the side. "Yeah, I'm free. I wasn't planning on catching up with my family until after the game tomorrow, so I can be there."

Blaine found Mason's reaction curious. He almost seemed as if he were hiding something, but he had no time to pry. "Thanks guys. I'm going to see who else I can round up. Think you can be ready in half an hour?"

The two men nodded and Blaine headed out of the room to see who else might still be around and willing to help out.

KENZI

Kenzi watched Shelby's face as she ended the call. Her friend had been so wound up today - first with the news about Tucker being involved in a bar brawl and then him not showing up to help plan the party he'd said he would pay for. For his sake, Kenzi hoped he had been the one on the line because if he didn't apologize soon, Shelby would tear him a new one when she saw him again.

Her best friend was not normally an angry person, but the kids at this center meant everything to her. And if she had to disappoint them, someone was going to pay.

"Was that Tucker?" Kenzi kept her voice light as she posed the question. She certainly didn't want to earn a spot on Shelby's bad side if the news wasn't good.

"It was. He said he left a message about today." Shelby's eyes roamed over the desk, and she lifted papers as if she expected to see a handwritten note somewhere. "Evidently his father had a heart attack."

Kenzi's hand flew to her mouth. She knew firsthand how serious heart attacks could be - her grandfather had died of one at the age of sixty-eight. "Oh my gosh, is he okay?"

Shelby paused her search and lifted her eyes to meet Kenzi's in a blank stare. "I don't know. I forgot to ask."

She'd forgotten to ask? How was that possible? Shelby was the poster child for courtesy and decorum. She always said "bless you" when somebody sneezed, sent thank you cards for every gift she received, and kept a stack of "get well" notes in her drawer for whenever the occasion might arise. Kenzi knew Shelby had been distracted lately, or perhaps consumed was a better word, with the center's rent and the Christmas party, but she couldn't believe she hadn't asked Tucker how his father was. She definitely had too much on her mind right now.

"Anyway," Shelby continued with a shake of her head, "he said he was sending me money through PayPal and that I was to take care of the decorations and to spread the word. He said he'd take care of the gifts."

Decorations? Money? The words were like manna to Kenzi's ears. "Well, we better get started then. We've got a lot to do before tomorrow night."

"Right. Why don't I transfer the money to you and you pick up the decorations while I start calling?"

Disappointment flooded Kenzi. She'd been hoping to spend a few hours with her friend like they used to - before Shelby took over managing the center and trying to carry the weight of the world on her shoulders. "Can't you come too? Just for an hour or so? It will be like old times."

"Kenzi, there's so much to do," Shelby began. The pinched look covered her face again.

"And it's not going anywhere," Kenzi said, interrupting her. "It will still be here when we get back, and I promise we'll be quick. I'd just like to spend some time with my best friend. Please?" Kenzi put on her best puppy dog eyes. Shelby swore she was immune to Kenzi's charms, and maybe she was, but more often than not, Kenzi could convince her to say yes with a few eye bats and a well-timed pout.

Shelby's face eased into a smile, and a small chuckle escaped her lips. "Okay, you win. One hour and then I have to get back to work."

It wasn't as much as she'd hoped for, but Kenzi would take it. Any time with Shelby outside the center felt like a gift and one she planned to make the most of.

"Okay, so I'll transfer the money to my account. That shouldn't take too long. It will probably take us about fifteen minutes to get to the store which leaves us approximately thirty minutes to shop. That is, of course, if we can keep our travel time under fifteen minutes because we'll need time to get back as well." Kenzi wasn't sure whether Shelby was talking to her or herself since her head was down and her gaze was focused on her wristwatch. "We need to make sure we're back in time to set up for the kids this afternoon."

Kenzi rolled her eyes good-naturedly. Shelby was nothing if not efficient, and Kenzi had never known her to mess up a schedule. Ever. "Don't worry. We'll have plenty of time. I've already got an idea of what I'd like to do."

Shelby glanced up with a look of surprise as if she'd forgotten Kenzi was even with her. "Right. That's good because you know me and decorating." Kenzi smiled as she opened the driver's side door. She did know Shelby's idea of decorating, and it was atrocious.

Shelby's mother had let her decorate her room when she turned sixteen, and as Shelby couldn't decide whether she preferred purple or red that year, she'd used both - on the walls, on the curtains, on the bed. When she'd finished, it looked like someone had massacred Barney the Purple Dinosaur in there. So, when Shelby had finally moved into her own apartment, she had called Kenzi to help her decorate it. They'd left the walls white, as most landlords didn't let you paint walls anyway, and used accents to bring color into the room. The effect was a much more subdued, cohesive atmosphere. Of course, it also helped that Shelby had finally decided on lavender as her favorite color. Kenzi shivered at the memory and turned the key in the ignition. "Yep, no decorating for you."

"Hey!" Shelby slugged her on the shoulder, but it was light and a smile graced her lips, so Kenzi knew she wasn't really mad. Besides, she'd been the one who brought it up. Not Kenzi.

"Simply Having a Wonderful Christmas Time" came on as Kenzi drove to the store. She loved Christmas, and this was her favorite Christmas song. Something about the beat stuck with her long after the song ended, and she would find herself humming or whistling the tune hours later, but she didn't mind.

Since the age of three, she had loved all things

Christmas - Santa, presents, the tree, but most of all the lights. There was something magical about Christmas lights, both on the tree and on houses at night. It transformed them, brought out magic and made them appear brighter, warmer, cheerier. No matter how cold, Kenzi loved to walk around the neighborhood after dark and stare up at the lights. Her imagination would create stories of the people inside - mothers in aprons baking gingerbread cookies, fathers in Santa hats reading stories to the kids, and the children bundled in footie pajamas drinking hot chocolate as they listened to their fathers read. Of course, her own childhood had been nothing like that, so she wasn't sure why that was the picture she created, but maybe it was *because* her own family had been nothing like that.

No, her family had been the other kind. The kind that paid people to come hang their Christmas lights because they didn't have time to do it. Or didn't want to make the time. And forget colorful lights or icicle lights - those were too impractical. Solid white lights were the only way to go. In a single solitary row, like good little soldiers. The tree was an enormous twelve-foot artificial tree that had been purchased before Kenzi was born, but her father never set it up. No, hired help did that too. And while Kenzi was allowed to hang ornaments, the maid was told to come in after and rearrange them all so that they were spaced evenly and uniformly apart. There were never stories or gingerbread men or hot cocoa, but still Kenzi loved it.

When she'd been old enough to earn an allowance, she had saved up until she could purchase a small artificial tree for her room. No one complained how she decorated that one. Every year, she would pull out her little two-foot tree the day after Thanksgiving, and after she decorated it, she would add her cheer to the rest of the house. Then, she would record all the Christmas movies and marathon watch them when she had time. She was determined that one day not only would she have a Christmas like they did in the movies, but that her parents would join her and enjoy it too.

Kenzi parked the car in the Wal-Mart lot, and they headed inside and toward the Christmas section. Several rows had been dedicated to the holiday and were over-flowing with ornaments, wrapping paper, and lawn displays. Kenzi knew exactly what she wanted though, and with the five hundred dollars Tucker had wired over, it would be more than enough.

3

BLAINE

Blaine could not believe all the toys Tucker had purchased. In addition to the five men he'd gotten to help him last night, another four had agreed to help out tonight. Tucker had returned with his former teammate, Emmitt Brown, so including Blaine there were twelve guys. Still it took them almost an hour to get all the gifts loaded up. Almost an hour and four trucks.

"Blaine, you wanna ride with us?" Tucker asked as the men began choosing their rides.

Blaine glanced around and nodded. Most of the other guys had already teamed up. Besides, he was curious about Emmitt. He held the door open and let Emmitt climb in first. Then he entered beside him and shut the door. A moment later, Tucker's door closed as well.

"This is a nice gesture," Emmitt said as Tucker turned the key.

"Thanks, Rev. I guess you rubbed off on me more than you or I knew."

Rev? Blaine wondered how the man had gotten that nickname. He would have to ask Tucker later. As they drove, he realized there was a lot about Tucker he didn't know. All he had seen before now was the confident running back with a chip on his shoulder, but here was a man going out of his way to bring gifts to kids he barely knew. Had it been the center that changed him so profoundly or something else?

"So, how's married life treating you?" Tucker asked.

A wide smile broke out on Emmitt's face. "It's the best, man. I can't believe I was so stupid and prideful at first not to see how amazing Mia was from the beginning. I still kick myself that I let so many years go by, that I missed Carter's birth." He shook his head and sighed. "Anyway, I hope one day you find what I have. Both of you. God said it was not good for man to be alone, and He was right. The two of them complete me in so many ways I never even thought possible."

Blaine wondered what the story was with Emmitt. Not only was he married, but he had a kid as well? He wanted to ask him if it was hard to balance a family with the requirements of pro-football - not that he was looking to start a family anytime soon or ever with his past, but it was still good information to know. He kept his mouth shut though. It didn't feel right to interrupt their reunion.

As Tucker pulled into the parking lot of the center, Blaine's eyes widened. He wasn't sure he'd ever been to the center, but it had been a long time since he'd seen this many cars anywhere besides the stadium on game day. There were so many that Tucker was forced to pull the truck into the fire lane.

"Are all these cars here for the party?" Blaine asked.

Tucker nodded and turned off the ignition. "I think so."

Emmitt chuckled softly. "I hope we brought enough gifts."

"Well, if we didn't, then I'll just have to go shopping again tomorrow."

Before anyone could say another word, a woman in red came barreling their direction. Tucker opened the door and climbed out.

"Who's that?" Emmitt asked, leaning forward to see around Blaine.

"I'm not positive, but my guess is that is the director. Shelby something or other."

"Is there something going on between them?"

"What?" Blaine looked again at the scene unfolding outside the window. Could it be? Was that the reason for Tucker's recent change? "I have no idea."

"I rather hope it is. He deserves to find someone."

Blaine glanced at Emmitt, wondering what he knew

about Tucker that Blaine didn't. Perhaps Blaine should have tried harder to get past Tucker's rough exterior. He would do better in the future. Being captain of the team meant responsibilities, and part of those responsibilities was knowing his teammates. "Shall we?" He nodded toward the window.

Emmitt nodded, and Blaine opened the door. To his right, he heard the sound of the other men opening their doors and climbing down as well. Tucker exchanged a few words with the woman in red and then she turned and strode into the center. A large smile adorned Tucker's face as he pivoted to face the players. "Let's go, boys," he said and motioned with his hand for them to begin unloading the gifts.

Blaine loaded one under each arm and followed Emmitt into the center. Christmas had lost its excitement for him years ago, but a tiny twinge of something still tugged on his heart as he entered the center. White twinkle lights hung in low loops from the ceiling along with red, green, and white streamers. Cheery wreaths of green and gold hung around the room like pictures frozen in time, and a small artificial tree completed the scene. The children had obviously decorated it as the ornaments were uneven - clumped in places and sparse in others - but somehow that only added to the magic. A table with food and drinks sat off to one side almost like an afterthought. Certainly no one was paying any attention to it at the moment. No, the attention was very clearly on the players as they entered with their brightly wrapped boxes.

A silence hung in the air for just a moment, and then one child spoke up. "It's Tucker. I knew he'd make it." That was all the encouragement the other kids needed. Like a giant wave, their energy washed over Blaine as little feet and eager faces scurried towards him. Memories of previous Christmases flooded him, and he forced them from his mind. He couldn't think about them now or he would lose it, and tonight wasn't about him. It was about these kids. Their voices spoke over each other as if a prize existed for whoever could be the loudest.

"One at a time," Tucker said with a smile, and he held up his hands to calm the children. "Let my friends set the gifts down first."

Like magic, the children quieted, but their energy did not dissipate. Instead, it zinged around inside each one like a pinball. Blaine could see it in the bouncing of their feet or the shifting of their eyes as they looked from one player to the next. He hoped Tucker didn't speak long because he felt like the invisible dam holding the kids back might break any second.

"First, let me introduce my friends."

Inwardly, Blaine groaned. This was exactly what he'd been afraid of. While he didn't mind introductions, there were twelve of them. He didn't think the kids would last that long. A movement to the side caught his attention, and the world around him seemed to freeze as he caught sight of a beautiful woman in a dark green dress.

Blaine was not normally one to fawn over a pretty face. He knew he was damaged, and he had no intention of dragging a woman into his mess. At least not long term, which was why football had become his wife and women had been a nice way to spend a Friday evening, but there was something about this woman that held his interest. Something that drew his eyes to her, and he didn't think it was just her looks. She was gorgeous, no doubt, with her dark hair and creamy white skin, but he felt there was something else. Felt? What was he doing? He was not supposed to feel anything when it came to women. Not only did he have nothing to offer a woman, but he would never be able to give a woman a family, so feelings were not allowed. He was supposed to ignore these feelings - swallow them and lock them away deep inside. It was fine to take a woman out once, for companionship, but feelings were not allowed. Ever! Not after the accident.

KENZI

Kenzi felt his eyes on her before she actually caught him staring. Tucker had managed to bring eleven teammates with him, and they stood in a line facing the children, wrapped boxes placed at their feet. Most were smiling though she could tell a few felt completely out of their element. They were easy to spot by their rocking motion or restless eyes. Her gaze traveled up the line, but it stopped when she realized one pair of eyes was staring back at her.

Deep and brown, they looked warm and inviting but also as if they contained secrets. Blaine Hollis. Of course. She'd found him attractive when the team roster had been first announced, but she'd been sure he had a girlfriend like most of the other players did. However, as time went on, she realized the one thing about Blaine that stood out was that he never had a woman on his arm. Or at least never the same woman. The television crews must have even caught on because they never panned to one in the crowd cheering him on, and there was never mention of one on news stories or in the tabloids. For some reason, he seemed intent on not dating seriously. Yet here he was staring at her.

Before she could react, his gaze slipped away and returned to Tucker who was explaining the rules of picking a present. The children rocked back and forth as if an invisible field kept them in place until he gave them the word, and then pandemonium struck. Kids raced to grab a gift and then began tearing into them. Cheers and gales of laughter filled the room, and Kenzi turned when a hand touched her arm.

Shelby smiled at her and then nodded toward the kids. "We did good, didn't we?"

"Yeah, you did." There was no way she was taking credit for this party. All of this work had been Shelby's doing.

"What are you talking about? This place is gorgeous, and it wouldn't have looked so amazing if you hadn't decorated it. I know you left college because you weren't sure what you wanted to do, but I think you might have found your niche."

Kenzi let the words sink in and gazed around the room. Maybe Shelby was right. She *had* enjoyed decorating the space, and it *did* look amazing. Could it be that she'd finally found her calling? "But, if I go back to school, how will you keep the center running?"

Shelby grinned and shook her head. "I don't think that's going to be a problem. I have a feeling this event will bring kids into the center, and once enrollment is up, I can hire more help if I need to."

"I'll think about it," Kenzi said, but her mind was already walking through the possibility. She'd enjoyed college when she'd attended until she'd realized she was taking classes she might never need. After changing her major twice and watching her graduation date move from four to five and then to six years, she'd decided she should save her parents some money and figure out what she wanted to do before taking any more classes. Kenzi had no idea what kind of degree an interior designer might require nor how many hours it would be, but it might be worth looking into.

When the commotion of opening presents began to die down, Kenzi moved to the refreshment table to help serve food and drinks. Her stomach rumbled as her eyes took in the delectable desserts, but she was not going to partake. Not only because the food was for the kids, but because she didn't need the sugar. People never understood when she told them that. "But you're so thin," they always said. "Surely a little sugar wouldn't hurt a little thing like you." But they didn't know about her past. They didn't know about the merciless teasing she'd endured in middle school and junior high or the rigorous diet she followed now to keep the weight off. Not even Shelby knew about that.

"Looks good."

Kenzi glanced up to see Blaine Hollis standing across from her. "Excuse me?" Surely, he had been referring to the food and not her.

A light pink color tinged his cheeks, and he shook his head. "The food, I mean. It looks good. Not that you don't, but-"

She should stop him, tell him she understood what he'd meant, but she was rather enjoying watching him try to recover. He always looked so cool and collected on the field. It was nice to know there was another side to him.

He took a deep breath. "Let me start over. The food

looks amazing. What would you recommend?"

Recommend? She could recommend nothing because she had tried nothing, but she didn't want to explain that to him because when she admitted the truth, questions always followed. "Well, if you like chocolate, the brownies are always a good bet, or if you prefer fruit, the apple pie has been a big hit."

"Which would you choose?" His gaze held hers, and a tingle ran down her neck at his boldness.

"Um." She licked her lips as she looked from the brownies to the apple pie. "Well, chocolate has always been my poison, so I guess I'd do the brownies." A part of her wanted to see him take a brownie, to know they had at least that in common. It wasn't much to build a relation- ship on, but it was a start, right? Relationship? What? She was getting *way* ahead of herself. The man was here for dessert, not to ask her out. But if they ever did go out, it would be nice to know they had a love of chocolate in common. Except - if he loved chocolate and ever offered her any, she knew she would take it because there was no way she was explaining to him why she avoided it now. And then where would she be? Maybe she wanted him to take the fruit after all.

"I guess it is a little like poison," he said with a chuckle, "but then that's why I work out so much. What's your name?"

"Kenzi. Kenzi Lanham." Her words felt tight in her

chest. She couldn't believe she was talking to Blaine Hollis. She didn't have a poster of him on her wall or anything - she was too old for that - but she did have a jersey with his name on it. Folded up and in her bottom drawer, but there. He was her celebrity crush, one of them anyway, and here she was having a conversation with him.

He nodded and reached for a brownie. His eyes stayed locked on hers as he took a bite. Kenzi held her breath, hoping she had made the right recommendation.

The corners of his mouth pulled into a smile. "This is delicious, Kenzi. You have good tastes. Speaking of, do you know who did the decorating around here?"

Kenzi's heart fluttered in her chest. He liked the decorating? Did that mean she really did have talent? "Actually, I did. It's not much, but it was rather last minute."

His eyes widened. "You did this? Are you a designer?"

Kenzi chuckled even as her teenage self screamed and swooned inside her. "No, not yet anyway, but," she looked again at the room, "I think I might be going back to school to get my degree."

"I think you should definitely consider it." He flashed her another smile though it didn't quite reach his eyes. "Well, Kenzi Lanham, it was nice meeting you. Perhaps I'll see you around?"

"Definitely." Kenzi held on to the lip of the tabletop to keep herself from folding to the ground as he flashed her a smile and then disappeared back into the crowd.

❄ 4 ❄

BLAINE

Blaine walked out of the Christmas party uplifted and also weighed down. It had been amazing to see the kids receive their gifts. Seeing them so excited had brought a smile to his face and reminded him of how much he used to love Christmas. It was obvious many of those kids had little money and didn't receive gifts often. That realization had convicted him, making him even more sure that volunteering and helping these kids out was important even if it pained him. As long as he never had to be solely in charge of them, he would be fine.

Then there was Kenzi. While he knew that would never amount to anything, it had been fun watching her and imagining, and that moment when she had licked her lips while studying the desserts had almost done him in. In fact, it had been a pretty perfect night until the text from

Coach. "The league is suspending Tucker for tomorrow's game."

Suspending. Blaine couldn't believe it. True, Tucker's anger had gotten him in trouble a week ago. After their last loss, he'd stopped at a bar to let off some steam and gotten into a brawl with a patron who antagonized him, but the bartender had said it hadn't been Tucker's fault. Tucker had even tried to leave, but the man wouldn't let him. No charges had even been filed. The Texas Tornadoes had decided that serving community service would be payment enough for Tucker, and he had served it diligently at the center, but evidently the other man hadn't felt that was enough.

He had complained to the league, and, wanting to make an example of Tucker, the league had suspended him for tomorrow's game - the biggest game of the season so far. If they won this game, they would move into the quarter finals, but if they lost, their season was over. Tucker hadn't been Blaine's favorite player to work with, but he was their best running back. And they needed him. Besides, it was obvious from tonight that Tucker was no longer the angry man he'd been a week ago. Something had changed him, and he deserved a fresh start.

"What's going on with you, man?"

Blaine glanced up at Mason who had offered him, Jefferson, and Rodney a ride back to their vehicles. "Just got a text from Coach that Tucker is suspended for tomorrow's game."

Shock and disbelief registered on the other men's faces. "What? How can they do that?"

Blaine bit the inside of his lip as he thought about whether he should share Tucker's secret. After the altercation, he and Coach had decided it would be best if they were the only ones who knew about it. Plus, it wasn't really his story to tell, but it had been on the news the night before. The guys might have heard about it already and perhaps if one man complaining could get him suspended, then maybe fifty men complaining could get him re-instated.

"Tucker had a recent run-in with the law. No charges were filed, but the guy he got in the fight with wasn't happy with that. I guess he complained to the league and they decided to make an example of him."

"We can't let them do that," Mason said. "I know Tucker has had his anger issues, but look at what he did tonight for these kids. He's not the same guy he was even a week ago."

"That was my thought too," Blaine said with a nod. "Maybe if we all call the league and tell them what he's been doing, we can get him re-instated."

Jefferson ran a hand across his smooth face. He was the baby of the offensive line, but his maturity often matched the older players. "I think I know of someone else who might be able to help. I overheard that reporter, Sylvie Sanders, talking to Tucker. She was asking him why the previous donor decided not to help out this year, but Tucker wouldn't say anything. I'm pretty sure he knows though, so maybe we can get her to do a story on it."

Blaine's mood perked up at that tidbit of information. "That's a great idea. Why don't you see if you can get her number while Rodney and I start calling the rest of the team. It looks like we're going to need a Christmas miracle."

KENZI

"Okay, that was a pretty amazing night," Kenzi said as she took down the last of the decorations still left on the wall. They'd been careful enough they would be able to reuse them again next year.

"Yeah, it was good," Shelby said, but her voice did not hold the excitement Kenzi would have expected. The woman had worked tirelessly to make sure this party happened, so why wasn't she happier?

"But?" Kenzi could tell something was up with Shelby, but like always, she was going to have to pry it out of her friend. Getting Shelby to open up sometimes was like trying to get a ship out of a bottle without breaking it.

Shelby set down the trash bag she had been filling with

discarded wrapping paper. "But I feel bad for Tucker. He did all of this-" she waved her arm around the now empty gym that had been teeming with delighted children earlier- "but because of Jude Renfrow, he's not going to get to play tomorrow."

"What?" Kenzi set the decorations down on the table and turned her full attention to Shelby. "What does Jude Renfrow have to do with this?" Jude Renfrow was a local businessman who had donated to the center last year, but Kenzi had always assumed he did it for the tax break and the recognition and not for the children. This year, he had decided to withhold his donation.

"Well, you know how I told you Jude Renfrow was the guy he got in the fight with?" Shelby folded her arms across her chest.

Kenzi nodded. This part she had heard before. She wanted to know why Tucker wouldn't be playing in the biggest game of the season so far.

"So, not only did Jude decide not to donate to the center this year because of Tucker, but when he found out Tucker had been working here, he called the league and got Tucker suspended."

"Can he even do that?" Kenzi followed football and knew suspensions happened, but they were usually for crimes or using athletic-enhancing drugs. "I didn't think one man could have that much sway."

"I guess one man with the amount of money he has can."

The words were filled with disdain as they left Shelby's mouth, but Kenzi couldn't blame her. Not only had Shelby grown up relatively poor, but she managed this center which existed to help the less affluent families in town. Money, and the right that some people thought it gave them, had always been a bone of contention for Shelby.

"Wait, wasn't Sylvie Sanders here tonight?" A wicked idea was forming in Kenzi's head.

"Yeah, why?" Shelby had no love for the reporter who'd made a pass at Tucker.

"Well, I happened to see her talking to Tucker earlier. Wonder what she could do if she knew the donor who left all these kids high and dry was the same man causing Tucker's suspension?"

The dots connected in Shelby's head, and her eyes lit up. "You're suggesting I tell Sylvie about Jude Renfrow?"

Kenzi shrugged. That was exactly what she was suggesting, but sometimes Shelby needed to think the idea was hers in order to execute it. "I'm just saying that if the league had that information, they'd have to decide if they wanted to please a business man or the whole community of Southlake kids who were treated to a wonderful night tonight by Tucker Jackson."

Shelby threw her arms around Kenzi and squeezed. "Kenzi, you are a genius. I'm going to call her right now."

Kenzi smiled as Shelby scurried away in her high heels, the hem of her red dress held high so as not to trip. Though Kenzi was normally the more persuasive one, she had no doubt that Shelby and Sylvie would accomplish lifting the suspension. Sylvie Sanders might be obnoxious, but she was doggedly determined. And she loved a good story.

Kenzi picked up the trash bag that Shelby had left and walked it to the large container in the kitchen. On her way back, she grabbed her bag from the refreshment table where she had left it earlier and opened it to stare at the ticket Shelby had given her earlier. Tucker had given Shelby two tickets to the player's box, and she had invited Kenzi. It was her own Christmas gift. Not only would she get to watch a live game - get to watch Blaine play - but she was going to get to do it from the fantasy suite.

The night of the Christmas party kept playing in Kenzi's mind as she followed her GPS to the address Blaine had given her for his cabin. That had been the night she met him, and though she'd only seen him a few times since, he'd played a starring role in her mind. There was just something about him that made her so curious. There was this hidden depth to him, something holding him back. She was both excited and worried about her mental health in taking this job. What if he hated what she did? What if she found out some horrible secret about him? There must be some reason he was a serial dater and had never ventured into a meaningful relationship. What if she found out the reason and it changed her view of him?

She gripped the steering wheel tighter. No, she could

do this. He might be the quarterback for the Champion Texas Tornado football team, but he was still human. He still put his pants on one leg at a time just like she did. At least she assumed he did. Unless he had a butler who did that for him, but did people have butlers these days? And if they did, did they really allow someone else to dress them? Good grief, her thoughts had the attention span of a gnat today.

The voice of her GPS brought her back to reality. "Turn right on Lost Lake Road."

Lost Lake Road. That was kind of ominous. She was getting close, though, and the thought sent her heart thudding in her chest. It was a beautiful road with gorgeous views. Blaine's cabin appeared to be rather secluded, so it would just be the two of them. Alone. Out in the middle of beautiful nature. Romantic, beautiful nature.

"Ugh!" Kenzi gripped the steering wheel as the car jostled her around again. Perhaps cruel, unpaved nature was a little more accurate. Lost Lake Road was hardly a road. Bumpy and unpaved, it wound through the middle of a growth of trees so thick that the sun above was obscured. She might even have to turn on her headlights to be able to see even though it was the middle of the day.

The contents of her lunch shifted in her stomach with the bumps, but finally she saw Blaine's red Mustang parked in front of a quaint cabin. It reminded her of the kind she used to build with Lincoln Logs when she was younger, only this one had flower pots sitting in the window sills and a chimney that she could imagine smoke drifting lazily out of on a cold winter night. A cold, romantic winter night.

The clump of trees nestled around it like they were guarding the cabin, protecting it, but Kenzi didn't get a scary vibe from it. More a feeling of tranquility.

She parked the car and checked her hair in the mirror. She'd spent an hour on it this morning trying to get it perfect, though the ride had undone some of her perfections. She didn't even know why she'd spent so much time on it. Was it because she was trying to get the job or trying to get Blaine? Maybe the two went hand in hand. After giving her cheeks a quick pinch to add a little more color, she grabbed her keys and her laptop and headed for the door.

Her spike heels immediately sank into the dirt. The sinking of her heels was not only coating her shoes and therefore her feet in dirt, but it was also offsetting her balance, giving her a stilted kilter of a walk up the path. She moved forward, putting most of the weight on her toes the way her mother taught her, the rest of the way.

The air was warm, but as she raised her hand to knock, she wondered if she should have paired a jacket with her dress. Did she look unprofessional without one? She was not used to second guessing herself so much. Her self-confidence wasn't high in every area, though she liked to pretend it was, but it hadn't been low in the area of fashion for quite some time. She'd found that love in high school and had often been the sought-after trendsetter. However, something about Blaine brought back the insecurities and fashion faux pas of middle school.

She ran her hand down her dress one more time to smooth any wrinkles before rapping on the heavy door. The sound of footsteps reached her ears a moment before the door swung open, and Blaine - looking easy in a t-shirt and cargo shorts - smiled at her.

"You made it," he said with an easy going smile that lit up his eyes.

A girl could swoon looking into those big brown eyes.

He leaned forward as if to hug her, but as Kenzi leaned in to meet him, he shifted his posture and the result was an awkward sort of shuffle that left her cheeks pink with embarrassment.

She shifted her eyes to her laptop as she tried to regain her composure. "I did. The directions were pretty clear, and my map app helped too."

"Great. Well, come on in." He stepped back to allow her entrance, and the masculine scent of him flooded her nose as she passed by. Dark and woodsy, she was unsure if it was his deodorant, cologne, or his natural scent, but what she did know was that it sent her heart thudding in her chest.

She wasn't used to a man having this sort of effect on

her. Normally, it went the other way. She would go out with a man she thought she was attracted to only to find out he didn't fit her ideal image after all, and she would end up breaking it off even though they seemed to really be interested in her. Was this what those men had felt like? This mix of nausea and elation? A feeling of regret flooded her; she certainly hadn't meant to make them feel this way. Though she was unsure if Blaine knew the effect he was having on her, she doubted it. He might avoid relationships, but he seemed like a decent guy.

The door closed behind her and then Blaine was beside her again. "Would you like something to drink? I'm afraid I only have water."

"Water would be fine," she answered as she looked around, following him to the kitchen. He must not use this cabin much if he didn't even have it stocked with drinks. The coating of dust on the bookshelves she passed bolstered that conclusion.

The kitchen was a small room with barely enough space for two people to maneuver. Cozy, but slightly claustrophobic, Kenzi chose to stay near the table. Made from wood, the table appeared sturdy enough to withstand decades, and the scratches and worn areas in the top led her to believe it had been around awhile. "So, have you had this place long?"

Blaine shrugged as he opened a cabinet door and pulled down two glasses. "It's been in my family for years, but I don't spend much time here." He looked around the room like he was looking for memories, that deep, dark look in his eyes.

There was more to that story, wasn't there? But he wasn't ready to tell her yet. He handed her a glass but didn't sit as he sipped from his own. He seemed uneasy. Was it her or the house?

"Would you like the tour?" he asked suddenly.

"Sure." Yes, he was definitely nervous. "Do you mind if I leave this here?" She motioned to the laptop she had set on the table. It wasn't heavy, but there was no reason to lug it around either.

"Of course." He set his glass down on the table and then held out his hand to help her to her feet.

She smiled at the gesture and placed her hand in his, but she was not expecting the heat that filled her palm. Her gaze caught his, and his wide eyes, before he dropped her hands, told her he had felt something unexpected as well.

"This way," he said as he shifted away from her.

The cabin wasn't fancy, but it was fairly spacious. He led the way first to the large master bedroom that lay to the right of the kitchen. A rustic looking bed and dresser were the only pieces of furniture in the room, but both appeared to be hand-crafted, adding to the charm. The carpet was worn but not threadbare, and while she would like to replace it if the budget allowed, she could work with it if it had to stay. Kenzi could envision a rustic retreat, somewhere to escape to. Calming and serene colors and cozy bedspreads. It could be gorgeous.

"What do you want to do here?" she asked as she walked around the room. She would take exact measurements later, but walking the perimeter always gave her an idea of the size she was working with. Plus, she would take pictures with her phone before leaving, in case she forgot anything.

"Honestly, I don't know. I'm probably going to sell the cabin when you're done renovating it anyway." Blaine leaned against the doorframe with his arms crossed.

"Sell it? But it's so beautiful and what an ideal place to come to get away from the hurry of city life." She couldn't imagine selling her family's lake house if she ever inherited it.

He shrugged. "I don't have much time to get out here with my football schedule, so there's no real reason to keep it."

"But what about your parents or other family members? Won't someone want to keep it in the family?"

"My parents never come here anymore, and there's no one else in the family who would want it." He bit his lip and frowned like he might want to tell her something, and she waited expecting him to put his thoughts together.

Instead he said nothing more, and his brusque tone and manner caught her off guard; she'd only ever seen him happy and smiling. This was a whole new side. "I get that."

He nodded and shook himself out of his funk. "So, what do you think?"

She looked at the room, her heart thumping. "Well, I was thinking of making it a place you could relax in, a nice little getaway. I have some ideas. Are you opposed to land-scape paintings?"

"No." He offered a tender smile as if realizing he'd been too abrupt before. "Whatever you think is fine. Really. I didn't have anything in mind; I just know it needs something."

"Great. After I see all the rooms, we can work out a budget."

He nodded and pushed himself off the doorframe. "Across the hall is the main bathroom. It's small, but it works."

Kenzi poked her head in and bit her lip. Small was an understatement. There was a tub with a shower attached, a toilet, and a sink. However, it was an old fashioned one, so there wasn't even a vanity with storage, and the pieces were so close together that someone standing in the middle of the room could touch all three. There wasn't much she could do with this space unless he was open to tearing down some walls.

"Over here is a small laundry room. It has an exit to the

back porch as well, so there's a place to take shoes off if they're muddy."

There was no washer and dryer in the laundry room. Only a basin and sink along with a shelf she assumed was used to fold clothes or hold detergent. She saw no other cabinets in the room. Okay, so running water but no washer and dryer. That might be a challenge, but then again, people probably came out here to get away, so maybe they wouldn't mind having to wash their clothes by hand. Or maybe they would pack enough for however long they planned to stay.

"I'm not sure I'll be able to do much with this room or the bathroom, but I'll put my thinking cap on."

He nodded. "I'll show you the outside in a minute, but let's finish the rest of the inside." He headed back into the main area where a terrifying staircase led the way to the loft upstairs. The steps were narrow and spaced too far apart. This might have to be replaced, especially if they wanted to appeal to families.

Upstairs there were another two bedrooms and a small bathroom, each decorated as simply as the master bedroom downstairs. At least it was a pretty blank palette to work with. In addition to the bedrooms, there was an open area that looked down on the main living room of the cabin. Kenzi could see it being a small playroom for kids or a comfy reading nook. She'd have to find out which direction he wanted to go.

The main room was easily the largest part of the cabin, but it had no soul. There was no color tying it together, no pattern, no preference of any kind, but she could see how it could be an amazing space. It was large enough to hold two couches and a chair as well as a coffee table in the middle. An ornate stone fireplace completed the look, and Kenzi could imagine curling up on one of the couches and watching the crackling fire for hours. If he were open to renting the cabin, she just might have to rent it a few nights herself. Maybe he would consider a night as part of her compensation.

"Ready to see out back?" he asked, breaking into her daydream.

"Absolutely." She felt warmth spread on her cheeks as she followed him back to the utility room. Had he caught her mind wandering?

"Well, out back," he said opening the door, "is the lake."

Kenzi stared in awe at the breathtaking view. She'd had no idea his cabin was on the lake. This would definitely offset the lack of a washer and dryer. Crystal blue water shimmered a mere twenty feet or so from the porch they stood on and stretched as far as the eye could see. Tall trees shielded every side of it, but the sun shone down in the middle, sending sparks of color across the surface. "Wow, this is amazing."

He only nodded, not able to bring himself to look at it.

His eyes stayed focused on her or the railing of the porch, never drifting out to the expansive blue beyond. Something must have happened here, but he was clearly not willing to discuss it right now. It killed her to think he would never enjoy this view, that this wondrous sight would be forever tarnished in his mind. "Well, it certainly is the cabin's best feature. It's gorgeous."

His answer was another shrug. He had shut down.

"Okay, well, I've got some ideas. Should we discuss the budget?"

❧ 6 ❧

TWO MONTHS PREVIOUSLY - BLAINE

Blaine stared at the cabin in front of him and sighed. He didn't want to be here - he'd never wanted to come back - but the cabin had been left to him. He still didn't understand why his uncle willed it to him instead of his parents, and while he could have refused it, he felt that would be a slap to his family. This was his responsibility now, and he could figure out what to do. And even though it was painful, maybe it was time too.

He sucked in a deep breath and inserted the key in the lock. He'd never been entrusted with the key before. The last time they had been here, he'd been only ten, and his parents hadn't trusted him with the key. Odd, how they'd trusted him to look after his brother but not with the small metal object.

The door creaked open, and the musty smell of

unopened rooms wafted out. Had anyone used this cabin since that winter? His family certainly hadn't been back, but his uncle had kids. Had they avoided it as well?

He stepped into the living room and tried not to get sucked into the memories. The blue checkered couch was exactly as he remembered it if not a little more worn and faded. That had been his favorite place to curl up when the fire was burning brightly in the large brick fireplace. The other couch - "his" place - also looked the same, and he could imagine him there, asking questions, hanging upside down, eating popsicles and getting messy and sticky like always.

Blaine crossed to the windows and lifted them open. He didn't plan to stay long, but the musty smell was over-powering, and the fresh air would help alleviate it. As he opened the window, a memory of it breaking filled his mind. He and Kevin had been playing baseball out front, and a wild tip had sent the ball careening into the window, shattering it completely. Not only had they gotten in trouble, but they'd had to pick up all the pieces of glass and replace it with their own money. That had been the last summer they played ball near the cabin. Ironically, it had been the last summer they'd visited the cabin.

The memories had been locked away so deep down for so long, only coming out in self-loathing and bad deci-sions. But being here - in this place where his presence was strongest - was bringing them all back. And it was rough. He'd even been dreaming about it again.

Blaine continued through the house, opening windows and checking for mice. Luckily, the cabin had remained almost preserved, like a mausoleum, and he found no traces of rodents. It did have a copious amount of dust covering almost every surface, and much of it was old and outdated. He would probably have to hire a designer to update it before he could sell it. He didn't really have time to be hunting for a designer, not with summer practice starting soon, but at least once the deed was done, he could get rid of the cabin. Maybe then the memories would disappear with it.

KENZI

At the buzzing in her pocket, Kenzi set down her lunch and pulled out her phone. She tapped the app and stared in disbelief at her email. The top one was from the Texas Tornadoes, but why would they be emailing her? Shelby was the center manager. She bit her lip and opened the email. Her eyes scanned the words, skimming over them and barely registering their significance until she got to the end. "Oh, my gosh!"

"What?" Her voice must have startled Shelby as the hand holding her drink jumped and liquid flew out of her cup, spilling the contents down her hand and onto the floor. "Darn it."

She set her cup down and stood to grab paper towels from the dispenser, but Kenzi barely looked up as Shelby began mopping up her mess. "I just got an email from the Texas Tornadoes. They want to hire me to redecorate the center and update it." She could not believe it; she was still finishing her degree at the college and hadn't even thought of putting out feelers for jobs yet. "They said they loved what I did for the Christmas party and want to do something special for the kids. They want me to do the whole center, and they're going to pay for it all and pay me on top of it."

Shelby tossed the paper towels in the nearby trash can and returned to her seat. "I knew it. I told you decorating was your thing. Now you have a job, and I'm sure more will come. In fact, I think we need to get you business cards so you can start handing them out."

Kenzi shook her head as she packed up her food. Lunch had felt too short, but that didn't dim her excitement. "Business cards would be silly right now. I don't even have my degree yet."

"But you will, and you want to be prepared when you do. Besides, it's my gift to you, and I refuse to take no for an answer." Shelby wadded up the rest of her trash and carried it to the dispenser.

Kenzi laughed at her best friend's insistence. She

wasn't sure who was more excited at this point, her or Shelby. "Okay, but can I have something fun and not just boring white?"

"Of course. I was thinking something pink and glittery."

Kenzi chuckled as she followed Shelby out of the small break room. "Do they even make pink and glittery business cards?"

Shelby glanced down at her watch. "I don't know, but we have a few minutes. We could jump online and check."

"Let's do it." Kenzi had no idea what this might mean for her future, but it definitely felt like a sign.

7

PRESENT DAY - BLAINE

Blaine groaned as the alarm blared in his ear. He loved playing football, but the early morning wakeups of training camp were definitely the worst part. The darkness felt thick in front of his face; the sun wouldn't be up for hours. He breathed deeply a few times to try and draw enough oxygen in to wake his weary body and then shut off the alarm. At least he had time for a hot shower before he had to head out. He knew people who could set the alarm and hit the snooze button two or three times, but he'd never been one of those people. When it went off, he was awake for better or worse.

Pushing back the covers, he swung his feet over the side and shuffled to the bathroom. Why did he feel so tired today? As he glanced in the mirror, he cringed at his face. Dark circles surrounded his eyes. He had clearly not slept well, but why? As if summoned by his thoughts, snippets of a dream flashed through his mind. Or perhaps nightmare was a more appropriate word. He saw himself laughing on the frozen lake, then the sound of the ice cracking changed his smile into a look of terror.

Blaine shook his head. He didn't have time to travel that road again. Nor did he want to. Thinking about the lake house had definitely dredged up some suppressed memories and emotions. He knew it had been a bad idea to go back there - he'd known it would bring up memories he didn't want - but it had to be done. Still, he had no time for this today. He needed to shower and get focused for practice.

An hour and a half later, Blaine pulled into the parking lot of the training center. The sun was just sending the first rays of gold and orange across the sky as he turned off the engine. Ten minutes until six. Perfect timing. He grabbed his bag and locked his Mustang before heading toward the door.

"Hollis, how's your summer going, man?"

The deep voice of Mason Dixon called out from behind him, and Blaine paused long enough to let his wide receiver catch up.

His summer. That was certainly a loaded question. His summer had been going great until he'd received the phone call informing him of his uncle's death. He hadn't seen the man in years, but he had been like a father to Blaine when his own father had grown distant. That had been distressing enough but then he'd gotten the call from the lawyer about the family cabin. Finally, he'd made the mistake of visiting the cabin, first alone and then with Kenzi.

And then there was Kenzi. He still didn't understand what was going on there, only that she lingered in his mind like no woman had. When she'd showed up at the cabin, it had taken all of his composure not to pull her in for a hug. He wanted to feel her in his arms - to see if she was the perfect fit he believed she was. He wanted to sniff her hair and find out if the sweet fruity scent that tickled his nose was real or just his imagination, but Mason didn't need to hear about any of that. Blaine had always tried to keep his personal life out of his professional life. It was better that way, so he swallowed these thoughts as well and shrugged. "It's a typical summer, I guess. How about yours?"

Mason nodded and shifted his bag higher on his shoulder. "Can't complain too much. Got to go home and see my family for a bit. Small towns though," he shook his head, "I'm ready to get back to work. You know what I mean?"

Blaine did. Training was exhausting, but it kept his mind from wandering to other things. Things from his past that haunted him if he dwelled on them. Mistakes he'd made, before and after the accident. "I hear you. I start to go stir crazy with too many days off, but I sure hope Glenn has added more to the menu this year than just oatmeal and eggs."

Glenn was the team's cook during training camps. He was a large muscular man who believed in only eating natural foods, but at least he was decent at seasoning the food so it had flavor.

"You and me both, man. I've been eating like a king, and I have a feeling it's going to come back to bite me." Mason pulled open the front door to let Blaine enter first.

Even if they hadn't known where the cafeteria was, they would have found it easily by following the noise. Having arrived close to the beginning of breakfast, many of the other team members were already inside and grabbing food.

Blaine dropped his bag by the door with the others and joined the line. It had been a while since he'd been in this training facility, but he was pretty sure there had been some major changes made. The serving line looked essentially the same, but off to his right was a smoothie bar area complete with blenders, protein powder, greens, and fruit. Past the serving line, he could make out a wood-fired oven. Did that mean pizza was possible this year?

"Is it just me or did they make some changes here?" he asked Mason.

Mason's eyes widened as if he was really looking at the space for the first time. "I think you might be right. I certainly don't remember a smoothie bar, and weren't the chairs red last year?"

Blaine looked to the seating area and smiled. The red chairs had either been replaced or recovered in a dark blue that matched their team colors. "Yeah, they were. Perhaps this bodes well for the food this year as well."

He was not disappointed. His heart lifted as he reached the serving line and spied the myriad of options. There were eggs and oatmeal but also omelets, steak, and even a fish dish. Evidently Glenn had stepped up his game, and Blaine wasted no time grabbing the steak and eggs. He hadn't thought he would be able to stomach eggs again, but paired with a steak, he could make it happen.

After filling his tray, he found an empty spot at a table and sat down. Mason sat down beside him, and a moment later, Tucker slid in across from him.

"How's engaged life treating you?" Mason asked when Tucker finished praying and raised his head.

"It's good, but, man, there is a lot to do for a wedding. No wonder women plan these things their whole lives. I had no idea the number of things that needed to be done." He shoveled a mouthful of oatmeal into his mouth, made a face, and then swallowed. "I have not missed this food. In fact, I'm pretty sure I haven't eaten oatmeal since the championship game until today."

Blaine took a bite of his steak and smiled. "Why did

you grab oatmeal with all the choices up there? This steak is amazing. Glenn must have been inspired or something."

Tucker raised an eyebrow. "You didn't hear?"

"Hear what?"

"Glenn left. He eloped with his girlfriend a few months ago, and they moved to California to open up some healthy bistro. There's a new cook now - some classically trained person - and I heard they hired like five other chefs to help out."

"Wow." How had Tucker heard about this before Blaine had? As captain of the team, it was his job to be informed. Of course, a few months ago was about the time he got the news of his uncle and the cabin, so it was possible he had heard and just forgotten or that the news had gotten lost in the shuffle. "Well, I hope they keep whoever this cook is around. I don't think I've eaten this well in a long time, and if there are this many options for breakfast, I can only imagine how good lunch will taste."

"I'll second that." Mason lifted his glass of orange juice into the air as if making a toast. A silence fell between the three men for a moment before Mason steered the conversation back to Tucker's upcoming wedding. "So, what are all the things you have to plan for that you didn't know about?"

"Why? You getting hitched soon?" Tucker asked with a teasing grin.

Mason snorted and rolled his eyes. "Doubtful. I just

want to be fully prepared just in case." His words were blasé, but Blaine noticed a shift in his eyes. Sadness? Regret? It appeared Mason might have a story he would need to flesh out one of these days as well.

Tucker took a drink of his orange juice and shook his head. "Man, it's crazy. There are invitations to pick out, and you can't just pick any invitation, it has to match the color palette. I didn't even know what a color palette was until a few weeks ago. Then there's the venue, flowers, cake..."

As Tucker continued to rattle off all the steps for planning the wedding, Blaine's mind wandered. He'd given up the idea of marriage a long time ago when he'd realized he couldn't be the protector a woman would need, but that didn't mean he never thought about it. He still had memories of when his parents were happy. When smiles and hugs were the normal behaviors instead of the angry voices and bitterness. Before the divorce. Before the accident.

No, he would not let his mind dwell on that. It was in the past, and it needed to stay there, and he needed to stay sharp. Focused. Training camp was hard enough already. He didn't need to be fighting demons along the way. And he didn't need to be obsessing over a woman. A very sweet, beautiful woman. A woman that made him feel like all his history and all his problems were fixable. He didn't need to be thinking about her, and yet, his mind kept going back to her.

He was a mess. A certified mess. And he still had to earn a paycheck, so he had to get his head in the game and keep it there.

KENZI

"Tell me again why you are picking out a dress so early. Isn't the wedding still a few months away?" Kenzi enjoyed shopping with her friend, especially since Shelby had taken a rare afternoon off from the center to do it, but she had just gotten engaged. Why was she already shopping for her wedding dress?

Shelby stared at her as if she'd just sprouted a third eye or something. "There's generally a minimum of six months to get a gown. I'm already pushing it with five and some change. Besides, Tucker and I want to be completely ready. January isn't that far away, and if we are going to pull this wedding off with a shortened time frame, we have to get everything in order now." She held up a lacy, cap-sleeved dress. "What about this one?"

Kenzi tilted her head as she tried to picture the dress on her friend. "I'd have to see it on, but I think a sweetheart neckline would look better on you." She shifted through a few dresses on the rack before finding what she felt might be the perfect one. "Try this one on for sure."

Shelby smiled as she added it to the rack of ones to try.

"So, are you going to tell me about the meeting with Blaine?"

Kenzi bit the inside of her lip. What could she say? The meeting had been... nope, there wasn't just one word for it. It had started off good when he'd opened the door with a smile, then it had turned weird as he gave her the tour of the house and refused to look at the lake. Finally, it had turned interesting as they went over her ideas and their hands touched. Yes, that's what she would go with. Interesting. "It was... interesting."

The squeak of hanger sliding against the metallic rack ceased as Shelby stared at her. "Interesting? What does that mean?"

Kenzi blew out a breath of air and shook her head. "I wish I knew. He was nice and friendly when I first got there. In fact, I thought he was going to hug me, but then he didn't and it turned kind of awkward. Then he showed me the cabin, but it was weird. He acted like he'd rather be anywhere else. This cabin sits right on the lake, but he wouldn't even look at it. And when I mentioned the amazing view, he just shrugged it off. Blaine definitely has some layers, and I'm never quite sure which one I'm getting."

"Okay, that is a little strange, but he hired you, right?"

"Yeah, he did. He said he liked my ideas, and we're getting together tomorrow to go over designs, but there was something off about him, Shelby. Something different than I've seen from when he's at the center." Her hand landed on the dress of her dreams. A picture of Blaine in a tux waiting for her at the end of the aisle as she wore this dress and walked to him filled her mind. What was she doing? She barely knew if the man liked her ideas, much less liked her.

Shelby's attention returned to the dresses, and the metallic creaking began again. "Well, maybe he was uncomfortable with it just being the two of you. Maybe he has feelings for you, but he doesn't know how to tell you and that's why he acted so odd."

Kenzi chuckled and smiled at her friend. Leave it to Shelby to jump to some romantic conclusion. Of course, she was doing the same thing. If only that were the case. She certainly wouldn't mind if Blaine showed a romantic interest in her, but if that was his idea of flirting, she had a lot to teach him. In fact, if that was his idea of flirting then maybe she could see why women only went out with him a few times. She'd always thought the reason was his choice, but maybe it was just him.

"What do you think of this one?" Shelby held up a beautiful white dress with a sweetheart neckline and iridescent pearls across the bodice. The dress picked up the light and reflected soft arcs of pinks and yellows. It was stunning.

Kenzi's smile spread slowly across her face. "That might just be the one. You ready to start trying them on?"

Shelby ran her hand down the white satin again and nodded. "I think I'll start with this one."

Kenzi sat on the pink, heart-shaped chair near the changing area and waited as Shelby changed. She had said she was going to model the last dress they had seen first, but she must have changed her mind because it was not the dress she stepped out in when the door finally opened.

This dress was pretty, but the neckline was far too high for Kenzi's tastes. Shelby was more reserved than she was, but this dress reminded her of eighteenth-century wedding dresses instead of today's current fashions.

"You're right," Shelby agreed as she looked in the full-length three-sided mirror. "This is a little stuffy."

The next dress she modeled was better, though still not her. Something in the cut just didn't flatter her waist the way it should have. The third dress got closer, but it wasn't until Shelby walked out in the last dress - the one they had liked even on the rack - that Kenzi perked up.

"Yes, I knew that was the one. Why'd you have to save it for last?"

Shelby smiled and turned a slow circle like Cinderella admiring herself before the ball. "I just wanted to be sure. I was afraid if I had tried it on first, I wouldn't have wanted to try on the other ones and then I would wonder if I really had the best dress. Now I know."

Kenzi rolled her eyes and shook her head, but she knew her friend was right. Shelby wasn't always decisive about clothes anyway, and her wedding dress was not something she wanted to waffle on. "Well, I'm glad you found it. Tucker will be swept off his feet."

"As will Blaine when he sees your ideas." Shelby's lips pulled into a teasing smile. "Now, when are you seeing him again?"

"Tomorrow after his practice. I'll finish up the designs tonight, and if he likes them, we'll start shopping and get to work next week."

"He'll like them because you're an amazing designer." Shelby stepped off the raised platform and linked her arm through Kenzi's. "Now, how about we find you your dress?"

8

BLAINE

Blaine sighed blissfully in the Epsom salt bath. After a long day of meetings, video review, weights, and finally practice, his muscles were tired and Epsom salts always made him feel better. He was no longer sure if the effect was physical or purely psychological from having done it so long, but he didn't care as long as the tension left his shoulders.

The alarm he'd set blared beside him, earning a groan from his lips. He'd promised to meet up with Kenzi to look over ideas tonight, and while he didn't mind seeing Kenzi again, he didn't really care what she did with the cabin. Once that cabin had held fond memories of summers at the lake, weeks when his parents weren't working and they relaxed as well, but that had been before. Before the accident. Before his world turned upside down. Now, he hated the place. He wished his uncle had sold it long ago, so he didn't have to walk down memory lane to do it himself.

He released a frustrated breath and pulled the plug. Another half hour would have been so nice, but maybe he could take another one after Kenzi left. He toweled off and pulled on his faded college t-shirt. It was too old and ratty to be seen in public, but he loved the comfort of it. It fit like a... well, not really like a glove. He knew that was the saying, but gloves had never fit his hands perfectly. His fingers had always been too long for most gloves. No, his shirt fit more like a perfectly worn-in pair of shoes - the kind that supported your foot in all the right areas, the kind that felt like you weren't wearing shoes at all.

The doorbell rang as he zipped up his jeans, and he ran a hand through his wet hair as he walked to the entrance to let her in.

Her eyes widened as he opened the door and she took in his still damp appearance. "Oh, was this a bad time? I thought we said seven, but I can come back." Her face turned pink with her flustering, and Blaine bit back a smile. He'd never seen her look so uncomfortable. Normally Kenzi appeared polished and sure of herself.

"No, you're fine. I just got out of a soak and I'm ready to see what you came up with." He hoped his words didn't sound as forced as they felt in his head. Honestly, if he could get paid to demolish the cabin, he would just do that. He stepped back to let her in.

"Okay, if you're sure." Her eyes scanned the large room. He'd purchased the house when he first signed with the Tornadoes, but he hadn't done much with it since then, and he was sure her designer eyes were cringing at the lack of style.

The room had matching furniture, but he hadn't gotten around to hanging anything on the walls yet - he wasn't even sure what he would want on them. Nor had he painted any of them; they still had the bright white that houses tended to come with so people could add their own style. His teammates all seemed to use designers or had wives or girlfriends that took on their houses. He just hadn't gotten around to it. Way too much going on all the time for him to set aside brain space for it.

"Wow, this is…" she paused as if searching for the right word, "big."

Blaine couldn't help the chuckle that escaped his lips. "Yeah, I guess it is and blank. One of these days I should do something with it."

He saw the spark in her eyes, and he wished he could see the images that were clearly flashing through her head. "Shall we set up here in the living room or the dining room?"

She looked toward the couch and her lips twisted in an adorable tilt. "Let's do the dining room if you have a table there. It might make it easier to see." Some sort of portfolio book filled her arms and a laptop bag hung off her shoulder.

He led the way through the living room and into the slightly smaller but no better decorated dining room. A large table that could seat ten took up most of the room. Blaine wasn't even sure why he had a table so large; he never had that many people over. Perhaps he should invite his teammates over more often; he certainly had the room to entertain them.

Kenzi set her laptop down on the table and opened the portfolio book, revealing paint chips and drawings and samples of fabrics. "Now keep in mind, you and this place are my guinea pig projects, so I need your feedback, okay? I don't have computer programs for everything yet, so I did a lot of the drawings by hand, but I brought my laptop so I could show you pictures of furniture and rugs if my drawings weren't enough."

The first sketch was of the master bedroom, and it was perfect. "Kenzi, this is amazing." She had found a way to bring life into the room without changing everything about it.

"I haven't even shown you everything yet. If you think this is gorgeous, wait until you see the other rooms."

She laid out the next board, and his jaw dropped. "Here's the living room currently," she said pointing at a picture she had taken of it, "and here's what I'd like to do."

Blaine stared at the images. The worn couches were

replaced with new brown leather ones. A masculine but romantic theme ran through the room with horns on the walls but candles placed on the mantle and the tables. Reds, blues, and browns were brought to life from the run in the center of the room and throw pillows on the couches. It looked comfortable but sophisticated, like it was meant to be lived in and enjoyed. He could almost see himself there, with family and friends, teammates and kids. It gave him a sinking feeling. No. No kids. And while he was at it, maybe no one else either. Just a good-looking place for someone to enjoy because he certainly couldn't. Not after what happened there.

He was overwhelmed. She ran him through the design. He touched the fabric swatches and took in the feelings that came with the changes she suggested. She was amazing. Even the way she talked was so soothing.

"Wow, that's pretty amazing." He knew it was the same room, the one where he'd played card games with his brother, where the two of them used to sit and read comic books, but it looked so different with Kenzi's touch. So different in fact that he wondered if perhaps he could spend time there again.

When she turned to him, he was surprised to see insecurity in her eyes. "You like it? Really?"

She looked so worried that he placed his hand on her arm out of reflex. He knew he shouldn't; he'd felt the jolt the last time he'd touched her hand, but he wanted to reassure her. He didn't want to be the cause of her doubt. "Really, it's great." The jolt was there again, humming beneath his fingers on her skin. What was it about Kenzi that affected him so? Normally he was able to turn off any feelings he might have for the women he dated, but something about her kept his defenses down, but could he really take a chance with her? No. He shouldn't. He shouldn't pull her into his messy life. It wasn't fair to her.

Her eyes held his for a moment. "Good, well, let me show you the rest." She dragged her eyes back to the portfolio and flipped another board. The two smaller bedrooms appeared and were similar in color and style to the master bedroom. His heart seized at the sight of the rooms he used to spend so much time in. Could he really sell the cabin?

"And finally, the kitchen." She turned the board over and he marveled at how she'd even managed to work the colors into the small kitchen. "I think we should replace the countertops along with the fridge and the stove, but the original cabinets are beautiful, so I just want to sand and refinish them."

He could barely believe it was the same kitchen. The yellowish countertop had been replaced with a beige and brown flecked marble that looked clean and somehow made the room appear bigger. "I always hated that countertop," he said with a slight chuckle.

"Can't say I was a big fan either."

She joined in with a smile and then caught his eyes

again. Their laughter faded as the connection between them pulsed invisibly in the air. He wanted to kiss her, to see if her lips felt as soft as he thought they must, but that was madness. He opened his mouth to commend her, but instead he bit down on his lip, looking too long at her mouth before she fidgeted in her seat and he looked at her eyes, feeling the heat. Too hot. Too close. "Would you like to have dinner with me tomorrow night?"

Shock registered on her face, followed by surprise, and then indecision. She probably knew of his aversion to dating and didn't want to get involved with that. Or perhaps she thought him a womanizer who went through women like socks - he knew there had been a few rumors floating around of that variety. Or maybe she just didn't date clients. Whatever the reason, he wished more than anything he could take the words back, but they hung in the air suspended by tiny threads as they waited for her to answer.

"I'd like that."

They were only three words. Three little words that could mean anything on a normal day, but coming from her mouth in answer to his question - he knew that they were going to change his life. Possibly forever.

KENZI

She'd like that? What had she been thinking? Yes, she found him attractive, but getting all flustered and distracted by his pretty eyes wasn't smart. Being attracted to him after accepting the job wasn't smart either. Plus, what about his reputation? Did she really want to be just one of the women he went out with a few times before moving on to something else? No, she didn't. She craved commitment, and she didn't feel he was ready for that, but it was too late now. Backing out now would be rude, and as she'd just secured payment for the job, it would be too uncomfortable.

With a sigh, Kenzi set her portfolio and laptop down on the passenger side and slid into the driver's seat of her car. She meant to go home, but she wasn't really surprised when her car pulled into Shelby's apartment complex instead.

Kenzi parked and bit the inside of her lip. Darkness had fallen while she'd been in Blaine's house, but it wasn't that late. Surely, Shelby would still be awake. Just to be safe though, Kenzi shot her a text as she walked up the walkway that led to her apartment.

The reply that she was always welcome came just as Kenzi reached the door. She knocked, expecting the look of surprise that covered Shelby's face when she opened the door.

"I was in the neighborhood," Kenzi said with a shrug.

Shelby smiled and pulled her inside. "So, what's going on?" she asked as they sat on the couch.

Kenzi sighed and dropped her head into her hands. "It's Blaine. I went over there tonight to show him the plans."

"And?" Excitement filled Shelby's voice.

"And he loved it."

"That's great. Why are you acting like that's not great?"

Kenzi lifted her head to stare at her friend. "It is great. I mean he actually relaxed, which was amazing, and he looked like he enjoyed my work…."

"As he should," Shelby said, interrupting her.

"Yeah, but then we had this weird moment."

Shelby's smile didn't fade as Kenzi had expected it would. Instead, one of her eyebrows lifted as she asked, "What kind of a weird moment?"

"Like a moment where he touched my arm like this." She demonstrated the motion, trying to have the same intense expression on her face that Blaine had, the one that made her squirm.

"Oh! That is something," Shelby said, fanning herself.

"I know!" Kenzi threw herself back on the cushions of the couch and covered her face with her hands. "And then he asked me out." She moved her fingers slightly to view her friend's reaction.

Shelby's eyes widened. "What?" A mischievous smile tugged at her lips.

Kenzi squeezed her eyes shut behind her hands and grimaced. "And I said yes." She lowered her hands and opened her eyes, expecting to see shock or dismay on Shelby's face, but she was grinning like a loon and staring expectedly at her.

"Okay, so what's the big deal?"

"The big deal is now he's my boss! What if it goes badly? What if it gets awkward? What if he forgets about me like he does all the other women he's seen? How am I supposed to keep working for him if that happens?" How could Shelby not see what a huge mistake this was?

Shelby placed a calming hand on Kenzi's arm and tilted her head down in the motherly gesture she had perfected. "Okay, first of all, you don't know why he doesn't see those women again. Maybe he goes out with them and realizes they aren't compatible. Second, what if it doesn't?"

"What?"

"What if it doesn't go badly? What if it doesn't get awkward? What if it actually works out? What if he didn't date those other women more than once or twice because they weren't the woman for him? What if it turns out God sent him into your life for a reason and you realize the two of you are perfect for each other?"

Kenzi both loved and hated this trait of Shelby's. On

one hand, she'd wanted her friend to commiserate with her, to tell her how awful this was going to be. After all, misery loves company, but on the other hand, Shelby was right. Maybe Blaine offering her this job had been at God's prompting though she didn't know if he were a believer or not. And maybe him asking her out had been the same. He'd certainly looked shocked when the words left his mouth, as if he hadn't planned them, but they had burst forth spontaneously. If that was the case, then maybe he could be attracted to her.

"Okay, maybe you're right."

Shelby rolled her eyes. "Of course I'm right. Besides, it's my turn to be the calming influence, especially after you helped me so much last year."

Kenzi chuckled. Shelby was usually the calming influence but the stress of finances and the lack of a donor during the Christmas season last year had sent Shelby spinning much the same way Kenzi was now, and Kenzi had been the voice of reason then.

"So, when are you going out with him?"

"Tomorrow night after he finishes practice." Kenzi tried not to let the excitement she felt flood her voice. It was one thing to feel it inside, but if she let it out then it might take control of her and she couldn't let that happen.

"You in a hurry tonight, Hollis?"

Blaine looked up to see Tucker just a few feet away. His hair was still wet from the shower, but he'd already gotten dressed.

"Yeah, I have a meeting with Kenzi Lanham." His eyes slid from Tucker's as he said Kenzi's name.

"A meeting or a date?"

Though he wasn't looking at Tucker, Blaine could hear the teasing tone in his voice. "Sort of both, I guess. She's redecorating this cabin I inherited earlier this summer, and I offered to take her to dinner." Actually, he'd asked her to dinner, but really the two were similar, right?

"Uh huh, and which does she think it is?"

Blaine swallowed and lifted his eyes to Tucker. "A date, probably."

Tucker laughed and shook his head. "Blaine Hollis and Kenzi Lanham. I can't decide whether that's a match made in heaven or a train wreck waiting to happen."

"What do you mean?" Blaine shut the locker and zipped up his bag.

"Look, I've spent more time with Kenzi than you have. I like the girl, but she's always seemed a little flighty. Sure, she's settled down more now that she knows what she wants to do, but only in her job. I haven't heard of her having a relationship since I met her. And then there's you. The man who's never brought the same woman to an event twice. You two are either going to be perfect together or set a record for who can run away fastest."

Though Blaine knew Tucker was right, hearing it didn't sit well with him. "You better watch it, Jackson. I can make practice extra hard for you next week."

Tucker Jackson held up his hands in surrender. "Hey, I'm just stating what I see. Really, though I hope you guys hit it off. Kenzi is a nice girl, and you both deserve a little happiness." With that he turned and exited the locker room before Blaine could say anything else.

He deserved a little happiness. The words ran through his mind like a broken record as he drove to pick up Kenzi. Was he giving off a vibe that he wasn't happy or was Tucker just issuing platitudes? And did he deserve happiness? After what he'd done? True, it had been years, but that didn't make the guilt any less real. Nor did it change the past.

The thoughts flew from his mind when Kenzi opened her front door. She was stunning. Her dark hair was pulled to one side and lay in curls down her neck and shoulder. The skirt she was wearing showed off her toned legs, and the smile she flashed at him seemed to brighten even the darkest places in his soul. "Wow," was all he could utter.

Pink sprouted on her cheeks, and her gaze dropped to the ground for just a moment. "Thank you. I'll take that as a compliment. So, where are we going?"

"There's a really great barbecue place I've been wanting to try out. How does that sound?"

She flashed a dazzling smile at him as she locked her apartment door behind her. "Blaine, I'm a Texas girl. Barbecue is what we do best."

He chuckled as he led her to his car, and he wondered just how much of a Texas girl she was. He'd never seen her in cowboy boots, but he could imagine she would make them look good.

"Are you really a native Texan?" he asked when she was settled in the car. Nothing about her, save a tiny hint of an accent, screamed Texan.

"Through and through," she said as he started the car. "I was Miss Southlake in high school."

Now that he could believe. Kenzi had the look of a homecoming queen.

"What about you?" she asked. "Are you native or an implant? I don't hear much of a drawl when you speak."

He chuckled as he pulled to a stop at the red light. "Native as well, and I used to have a thick accent, but when I began doing interviews, the coaches told me I needed to get rid of the accent so people could understand me. Took a few lessons and a lot of speaking with a pencil in my mouth, but I finally broke it."

Kenzi's forehead wrinkled as she stared at him. "A pencil in your mouth?"

"It's supposed to help you enunciate," he said with a laugh as he remembered his drama teacher making them all read their lines with pencils in their mouths. He hadn't really wanted to take drama, but it satisfied a fine art requirement and he had actually enjoyed it.

Kenzi joined in with his laughter. "I guess I'll have to try that sometime."

He shot her a quick glance before turning his focus back to the road. "Don't you dare. You have a beautiful voice just the way it is."

She smiled, and he enjoyed the soft pink that graced her cheeks again as silence fell between them again.

The restaurant wasn't overly crowded for which he was glad. He wanted to spend some time getting to know Kenzi. The hostess led them to a table in the back, and Blaine held out the chair for Kenzi as she sat.

"Thank you."

After he sat, the hostess left them with menus promising the waitress would be back soon to take their order.

"So, you said I would be your first real client after the center? Do you have any other jobs lined up?" The light from above cast a soft glow on her face which made her eyes seem to sparkle and shimmer, and he was having a hard time making his brain process even simple statements.

Her teeth chewed lightly on her bottom lip. "I had a few interviews last week, but I haven't heard back from any of them." Her eyes darted to his. "I hope that doesn't make you reconsider hiring me."

Blaine wondered where this lack of confidence was coming from. From what he'd seen, she was amazing, and he had no doubt he would be pleased with her work. "Not at all. I have no doubt that your business will take off, especially after seeing your designs. I'll help in whatever way I can."

"Thank you. I appreciate that." She paused and took a sip of her water glass, but he could sense that she wanted to say something more.

"What is it?"

"It's probably none of my business, but I am curious."

Curious. Now there was a dangerous word. What exactly was she curious about and was he willing to answer her question? Normally, now would be the time that he would shut down and deflect the question away, but he found himself opening up instead. "What do you want to know? I'm an open book." Well, mostly open. He wouldn't discuss his brother, but he doubted she would know about him anyway.

She considered him another moment before tilting her head and asking, "How is it that you're still single? You have this amazing job and this great personality, but I've never heard of you being in a relationship." Her eyes held his gaze for another moment before slipping to the side.

He should have known this question would come up, and while it wasn't an easy one to answer, it was definitely better than discussing his family. He shrugged, his eyes flitting around the room while he tried to come up with as much of the truth as he was willing to share. "Well, I guess I just haven't found a woman I wanted to spend a lot of time with." That wasn't a total lie. "You know I could ask the same question of you."

A knowing smile crossed her face. His change of subject hadn't gotten past her. "Yes, I guess you could, and I suppose my answer would be very similar to yours. I've been told I'm a little picky."

"Well, I hope you're not so picky that you can't find something you enjoy on the menu."

"I don't think that will be a problem at all."

It was odd how comfortable he was around her, how he could laugh and joke with her. He couldn't remember ever feeling like this around a woman. And it scared him to death. Eating with her was nice. Spending time with her was refreshing. He could see himself falling for her, but what if he couldn't protect her when she needed it? He wasn't sure he could live through the past again. Nor could he imagine spending another lonely night at home knowing he could have a night like this.

KENZI

Kenzi could see the invisible wall Blaine kept up lowering as the night went on. She wasn't sure what he kept the wall up for, but she was certainly enjoying getting to know this side of him. He was funny and caring and she could feel herself falling for him even though she kept reminding herself that she couldn't. Her brain knew there were a million reasons she couldn't, but her heart just didn't seem to agree.

It was her heart that spoke as she set her glass down. "If you have time tomorrow, would you like to come with me to pick appliances?" The words flew past her lips before they registered in her brain, and she hoped they didn't dampen the mood. She didn't want him to think she only cared about business, but she did want to see him again. This would be a perfect opportunity. She clamped her lips shut as she waited for him to answer. The need to explain her reasoning thudded in her brain, but she figured it would be safer to hear his answer first.

His eyes twinkled as he regarded her. Darn her face and its inability to mask her emotions. "What would that entail?"

His teasing response caught her off guard. She had expected him to make an excuse as to why he couldn't, not flirt with her across the table. "Um, well, I like to save money on appliances because I usually need it for other areas, so I generally buy them at Home Depot. So, I guess that would entail meeting me there and helping me decide on which appliances."

"And is that all it would entail?"

All? What was he asking? Did he expect to get a massage after it or something? "I don't know what you mean."

He smiled at her obvious discomfort, and a tiny dimple appeared in his cheek. Was he razzing her?

"How about this? I'll help you pick out appliances if we can have dinner again afterwards."

Dinner again? Kenzi's head was spinning. Blaine, the guy who never saw the same woman twice, wanted to have dinner with her two nights in a row? She should say no. Her mind knew that much. This was too weird, too unlike him.

What if this was like fifth grade when Brian Harding asked her out in a note at lunch and sent her little heart thumping in her chest? Brian had been her first crush, and the thought that he - one of the most popular boys - would like her when she wasn't the thinnest or the cutest or the most popular girl had been more than she could bear. She'd floated through the next few classes until they had social studies together, but when she'd entered that room and told him her answer was yes, he laughed it off and told her it had all been a joke. It hadn't been funny to her, and the next day he was seen flirting with Wendy Wiseman - the thinnest, cutest, most popular girl in the fifth grade. A part of her had died that day, and she never wanted to feel that way again. So, what if she said yes and then Blaine never showed?

She knew there was danger here, but that didn't keep her mouth from saying, "Okay, dinner sounds good."

"Good. You ready to get out of here?"

He stood and held out his hand to her. Had he already paid? How had she missed the check coming? Was this a date then since he'd paid? Even more importantly, was tomorrow a date? Kenzi prided herself on being in control, but right now, she felt like a kid on roller skates for the first time. The only thing she was sure of was that she was enjoying spending time with Blaine and she didn't want it to end.

Placing her hand in his, she let him pull her up. She expected he would drop her hand as soon as she was on her feet, but he didn't. Instead, he gripped her hand tighter as he led her out of the restaurant.

"You feel like a walk?" he asked when they exited the restaurant and the cool evening air hit them. It was almost eight and the sun was setting in the sky, sending brilliant oranges, reds, and pinks across the sky. She'd visited a few other states, but there was nothing like a Texas sunset, and she couldn't imagine seeing it a better way.

"Sure."

He led the way away from the restaurant and down a lighted path. Kenzi's gaze dropped to their entwined hands every few minutes. She still couldn't believe she was on a date with Blaine Hollis. Nor could she believe he was holding her hand. It was too bad Brian Harding couldn't see her now.

The silence between them wasn't strained, but Kenzi had so many questions. "When did you start playing football?"

"Young. I used to play..." he paused and his jaw tightened, "with my dad in the yard. Then I began playing for school in the seventh grade, and it just went from there."

She wondered what that pause had been about. Did he not have a good relationship with his father? Had it soured for some reason? She realized she knew nothing about his family. Even when he was interviewed, Blaine always shifted the focus away from his family and to the game. She was no detective, but something was definitely going on there. "So, did you always want to play professionally?" Kenzi knew it was a common desire for young boys. Many at the center had listed that as their dream occupation when asked.

The vein in his neck bulged and his eyes slid away from her. "Yeah, pretty much."

A follow-up question burned in her throat, but before she could ask it, the sound of children's voices came their way.

"Kevin, wait up."

"No, you're being a bully, and I don't want to play with you anymore."

Blaine tensed beside her, and his hand turned clammy against hers. The two boys rounded a corner and hurried past them with barely a second glance, but even after they were gone, Blaine remained rooted to the spot.

"Are you okay?"

He was silent a moment and then shook his head as if clearing away some memory. "I'm fine. Let's just go."

His gruff demeanor had returned, and as he turned around, he dropped her hand as well. Kenzi missed the warmth it had provided, but more than that she wondered. Why had the two boys affected him so badly? Had he known them? They had been having such a wonderful time, and then all of a sudden, it was over. She missed the feeling of his hand in hers.

❧ 10 ❧

BLAINE

Blaine took a deep breath as he parked in front of the Home Depot. He should never have suggested this; he'd let himself get caught up in the moment with Kenzi last night. He'd held her hand and let himself think about the way she smelled and how soft her skin was. He'd let himself believe that maybe he could have a relationship, and then that dream had been shattered when he'd heard the name. Kevin. The sound of his brother's name from the young boy's lips had drawn him back to the past faster than a bullet train.

The two boys had come around the bend, and Blaine knew they had to be brothers; they looked so much like he and his own brother had at that age. As he'd watched them, he'd seen, for just a moment, a similar time from his past. A time when he'd wanted to run through the forest and his brother had been afraid and hung back. He'd goaded his brother in much the same way as those boys last night, and that memory had reminded him again of his failure as a protector. He hadn't protected his brother then, and he couldn't protect Kenzi or anyone else now.

He took another deep breath, dreading this meeting, dreading seeing the worry and confusion on her face like he had last night. Unfortunately, he had already issued the invitation before the painful reminder came, and now he had to follow through. Bailing on her would be rude, and he couldn't bring himself to do it. He would just have to keep his distance and remain strictly professional with her, but that was easier said than done. He really liked her.

It had felt good holding her hand last night. So good that for a time he had forgotten he couldn't have that for real. He could pretend for a night, maybe even two - heck, he was used to that - but she deserved more. She deserved someone who could always be there for her, and that just wasn't him.

He locked the Mustang and headed toward the front entrance. Kenzi was there already, her long dark locks piled on her head. Her top hung crooked, baring one shoulder completely, and her tight jeans showed off her toned legs. This was going to be harder than he thought.

Her lips split in a wide smile when she recognized him. "You made it."

He nodded, wondering if he could feign illness to get

out of having dinner with her. It wasn't that he didn't want to have dinner with her, he just didn't trust himself to have dinner with her again. She had a way of getting him to lower his walls, and he needed to keep them firmly in place.

Her smile faltered a little as if she'd expected a different greeting, but she kept her composure. "Shall we then?"

He followed her inside and tried not to think about the disappointment that had flashed across her face momentarily. It was better this way, and if he could just keep himself from flirting with her, then maybe they could go back to the way it was before he asked her out, before he held her hand, before he felt his heart thaw in his chest.

"So, where do we start?" He was careful to keep his eyes focused on anything except her face as he spoke. If he looked in those eyes for too long, his resolve would fade, and he couldn't let that happen.

She flipped open the notebook she'd been carrying under her arm. "Well, I thought we'd start with the oven and the fridge. They're the biggest purchases by far. Then, we can look at vanities and paint."

"Okay, lead the way." Blaine was careful to let her stay just a bit ahead of him to minimize the chance of them locking gazes. Still, he couldn't help but think about what it would be like to shop with her like a real couple. Would she take charge like she was now or would she defer to him and let him help make decisions?

"Based on your space, I've already narrowed down the options. I tend to think Stainless Steel will look the best, but I believe they also carry ones in cream or black that would fit your space."

Black? He couldn't imagine a black fridge and cream sounded like it would show dirt easily. He didn't know who might be buying the cabin, but if they had kids anything like him and his brother when they were younger, they would probably appreciate the Stainless Steel. He smiled slightly as the memory of peanut butter handprints on the fridge and cabinet doors flew to his mind.

"Blaine! Kevin! What is going on here?" Their mother stood in the kitchen doorway, hands on her hips and fire flying from her eyes.

"We wanted to make peanut butter toast," Blaine said.

"On the cabinets?" She threw her hands up in exasperation. "Did you have to touch every surface?" She reached on top of the fridge for a tub of wipes. "I'll be cleaning this for hours."

"Sorry, Mom," Kevin said. His big brown eyes filled with tears and Blaine knew they were going to rocket down his cheeks any minute. Kevin was definitely the more emotional of the two of them.

Their mother sighed. "It's okay, Kevin. Why don't you

boys go out and play while I clean this up and get dinner started?"

"Sure, Mom." Blaine, having finished his toast, wrapped his arm around his little brother and headed for the back door.

"But stay away from the lake," she called after them as they exited the cabin.

Blaine squeezed his eyes shut to push away the painful memory. That had been one of their last summers spent at the cabin. "I think I agree with you on the Stainless Steel."

She turned his direction faster than he could shift his gaze, and her eyes caught his. Darn it; he was trapped now. "Great, Stainless Steel it is. Do you think the same for the oven?"

He wanted to look away, but there was something in her stare that held him like a tractor beam. What was it? As he looked into her eyes, he suddenly knew. Questions and self-doubt swam in there beneath her confident bravado, and he found his wall lowering again. He wondered what had happened to her to make her second guess herself so much. "Yeah, I think whatever you think will be amazing."

Her lips pulled into a tight line and tiny lines erupted on her forehead as her brows pulled together. "What's going on with you, Blaine?"

"What do you mean?"

"I mean last night you were all smiles and laughter and hand holding. You agreed to come only if we could have another dinner afterward, but now you're acting as if you'd rather be anywhere else. If you've changed your mind about having me decorate the cabin..."

"No." He grabbed her arm to stop her derailment; he couldn't let her doubt herself. The touch of his fingers stopped her voice, but it also sent pulsing waves up his arm. "It's not that at all, Kenzi. You know how you asked me why I've never had a relationship?"

She nodded but said nothing, waiting for him to continue.

"Well, the reason I haven't is because I can't."

Her face furrowed in confusion. "What do you mean you can't?"

"I mean physically I can, I guess, but..." He sighed. This wasn't coming out right at all. "Something happened in my past that keeps me from connecting emotionally. Does that make sense?" He hoped she wouldn't ask what because he wouldn't go into details. Couldn't go into details. They were too painful, and they needed to stay locked away in his mind.

"A little, I guess. Something happened that made you think you don't deserve a relationship?"

Yes. She understood. Relief flooded him and he grabbed her other arm. "Exactly."

Her eyes softened and compassion filled her face. "Blaine, you deserve happiness. I don't know what's in your past, but it's the past. It doesn't have to define your future. There are things in my past as well, but God forgave me of all of them when I gave my heart to Him. He will do the same for you."

Her mention of God caught him slightly off guard. He supposed he should have guessed she was a believer. After all, Shelby and Tucker were, but he still wasn't used to people speaking so frankly about God. No one in his family had mentioned God since the accident, and he wasn't sure God would forgive him for what he'd done. "You might be right. I do feel differently around you, but I don't know if I'm ready."

"Okay, let's just get to work then." She slipped her arms out of his hold and turned toward the ovens.

"Wait, Kenzi." She stopped and turned to him. "I'd like to try though."

She frowned softly. "You'd like to try what?"

All the feelings of guilt and outrage at himself flooded him. He probably couldn't do it. He would have to acknowledge and own up to his mistakes first, and he didn't know if he was strong enough to do that. It was easy enough to pretend he was a relatively good person with a past, but opening himself up to let people see how truly horrible he was-- that took courage he didn't have. Not now. Not yet. "I'd like to try to be honest, and forgive myself. To give it to God and let go." He looked into her eyes as she stood there frowning. He picked up her hand. "If you can be patient with me, then I'd like to try. And if I can't, then you're better off without me anyway. I like you. I like being around you."

Her eyes searched his, and he willed her to say something, anything. Finally, her mouth opened, "I like you too, Blaine. If you can be honest with me, then I'd love to try to."

KENZI

Kenzi smiled as Blaine laced his hand through hers. She had thought he was going to break things off before they even really got started, but then he'd said he wanted to try a relationship. With her. On one hand, she was delighted and astonished. She'd had a crush on Blaine for years and he was willing to take a chance with her, but on the other hand, she was terrified. He hadn't had a real relationship ever from the sounds of it, and she wasn't sure she wanted to be the guinea pig. Of course her track record wasn't much better. After her last serious boyfriend wasn't there when she needed him, she hadn't dated anyone seriously either. It hit her then that his situation might be similar, and she should give him the benefit of the doubt.

"So, ovens?"

"Huh?" She looked over to see him grinning at her, and that's when she realized she had been standing in the middle of the aisle holding his hand but not moving. Probably looking like a dazed and confused moron. "Yes, ovens. Every kitchen needs an oven." She turned that direction and tried to focus on the task at hand, but the warmth of his skin against hers kept pulling her mind off track.

"Or a barbecue grill. This is Texas after all."

Kenzi shook her head and nudged him with her shoulder. "You can't have a barbecue grill in a house. Especially not that cabin. The whole thing would go up in smoke."

His lips split in a wide smile. A natural smile. The first natural smile she'd seen on him. "I didn't mean in the house. Just on the property. If I have a grill, I don't really need a stove."

"Ew, what about breakfast?" Kenzi loved barbecue as much as the next Texan, but there was a time to grill and there was a time to bake. A grill couldn't make all of the foods in her dietary rotation.

"Steak and eggs."

"Eggs on a grill?" That not only sounded disgusting, but how in the world did he keep them from falling through the cracks?

"Yep, a little tin foil and you're good to go."

Tin foil? She shuddered at the thought of the flavor of eggs cooked in tin foil. "Remind me not to let you make breakfast." The words died in her throat as she realized the innuendo she had just thrown down without meaning to.

Great, now what did she say? She glanced at him, but he seemed unsure of how to respond as well.

"Anyway, your cabin needs a stove. We're pretty tight on space, so really I just need to know if you want a flat top or the traditional kind?"

"I'm not sure I have a preference, so I'll let you decide."

Kenzi nodded and picked out the oven she had been eyeing online. "I think this one will go well with the plans I have for the kitchen. Okay, fridge and oven down. Now, we just need a vanity and paint."

"For the bathroom?"

Confusion threaded his voice, but she couldn't blame him. The bathroom was tiny and fitting a vanity in there would be a squeeze. "Yes, the vanity is for the bathroom. A woman is going to want some counter space and a drawer or two underneath to store necessities. We just need something thin enough to fit the small area."

His eyes betrayed his doubt, but he motioned for her to lead the way.

The bathroom vanities left a lot to be desired, and after measuring all of the ones that looked small enough, Kenzi sighed. "None of these will work. I may have to hire a carpenter."

"Maybe I could help with that."

She tilted her head as she regarded him. "Are you a carpenter too?"

"I am a jack of a lot of trades, but yes, carpentry is one of them."

Kenzi shook her head in surprise. There was definitely more to Blaine than he let on, but she supposed she could see him as a carpenter. He had the rugged build of someone who worked with their hands, and she had felt a rough patch or two when they were holding hands.

"Okay, I may take you up on that."

"Great. So, paint?"

"Yes, paint. I don't want to do much to the living room due to the exposed wood, but the bedrooms could use some paint."

"Paint it is then," he said, leading the way to the colorful aisle.

Kenzi perused the many colors, finally deciding on a dusty tan and a pale blue. The tan would be for the master bedroom, and she would bring in the blues with pillows and bedding. The upstairs rooms would be opposites - blue walls and tan accessories.

"Okay, we have a fridge, an oven, and paint. What's the next step in the decorating process?"

She placed a finger to her lips as she thought. She did want to discuss the carpet with him, but was now the right time?

"What? I can tell something is on your mind."

"I was hoping maybe we could talk about ripping out the carpet and putting hardwood floors in? It would really add charm to the place. Not that it's not charming," she added quickly.

He smiled and shook his head. "Don't worry, I get it. The carpet is old and looks worn. In fact, in some places, it is worn."

She tilted her head at him and waited for him to elaborate.

"I happen to know there is a small burn in the carpet of one of the rooms upstairs from a reading lamp."

"A reading lamp? How does that cause a hole in the carpet?"

Blaine scratched at his chin and averted his eyes. "Well, if the lamp has an adjustable neck, and it's a little old so it doesn't always stay up. And if a boy fell asleep while reading, it might be possible for the lamp to fold and the light bulb to heat the carpet enough to burn a hole in it." He turned a sheepish gaze on her and shrugged his shoulders.

Kenzi bit the inside of her lip to keep from laughing at the visual. "I wouldn't have taken you for such an avid reader, Blaine Hollis."

"Well, when it's night time in a cabin with no TV or video games, books have their appeal."

She batted his arm playfully. "Books always have appeal. Okay, so hardwood floors are a go. I'm glad because they're so versatile. Plus we can get a few ornate rugs because I'm sure the floor gets cold in the winter."

The muscles in his face tensed slightly, but then his smile reappeared. "It certainly does. So, let's get some hardwood."

Kenzi was surprised that Blaine had agreed so easily. True, she was the designer, but she always thought clients would be opinionated about aspects and push back. Blaine seemed to be completely the opposite. Whether that was because he had the money and therefore wasn't worried about the price or because his desire to sell the cabin was so strong, she wasn't sure. However, the more she interacted with him, the more certain she became that something had happened at that cabin in his past.

With the hardwood picked and ordered, Kenzi led the way to the front of the store to check out. "Okay, so now we need to check out and set up a delivery time for what we have here, and then I'll need to get out there and remove the current appliances and furniture, so we can do the floors and then move the new appliances in. Then I'll work on the colors - pillows, bedding, and the like."

A grimace crossed his handsome features. "I'm not sure I'll be much help with colors. I'm color deficient."

"Color deficient? Like you can see some colors but not all of them?"

He nodded. "I wanted to join the Air Force and become a pilot when I graduated, but one day they did one of those color blindness tests in school. Turns out I can't distinguish between some shades of brown and green, so flying was out."

"But you can still play football?" If he had issues with browns and greens, she wondered if he ever had issues with the ball and the turf.

He chuckled and his eyes twinkled as he regarded her. "Notice that I only throw the ball though. I don't catch it."

Her eyes widened. "So, you would have issues if you had to catch it?"

His laugh deepened, and she didn't think she'd ever heard a sweeter sound. There was a low rumble to it that reminded her of s'mores and warm camp fires. "Not like you think. I can tell the difference between the ball and the ground, but if I were a wide receiver, I might have issues seeing the ball as it flew through the air."

"Oh." She felt stupid though it wasn't like she had any experience being color deficient or playing football. She was a sideline cheerleader only.

He placed a finger under her chin to lift it in order to get her attention again. "Don't worry. You aren't the first person to ask me what it's like. I think I've heard every question by now."

His eyes were like a magnet, drawing her to him and making it impossible to look away. They say eyes are the windows to the soul, but Kenzi couldn't decipher what she saw in his eyes. Desire, fear, joviality, anxiety. It was like for every positive emotion she saw, a negative one existed as well. What had happened to him in his past?

His lips parted, and for just a second, Kenzi thought he was going to kiss her right there in the middle of the store. Instead, he dropped his hand and leaned back. "Shall we check out and grab that dinner then?"

Kenzi swallowed the disappointment flooding her body and forced a smile across her lips. "That sounds nice."

11

BLAINE

Blaine pulled up to the center and took a deep breath. He could do this. He could be around these kids. They weren't his sole responsibility, and they deserved this. His issues weren't their fault. The words were easy enough to say, but they were a lot harder to believe, especially with his memories from the past flooding him more and more often.

Even though things seemed to be going better - he'd actually been out with Kenzi twice now which he was pretty sure was a record for him - he knew that one familiar word, one specific memory could send him spiraling back down again. He'd felt it when he looked at the one picture he still had, a picture of them together at the lake.

"I'm going to try and make it work," he'd told the boy in the picture next to him. "I don't want to end up alone." The boy had said nothing, but Blaine was certain he'd felt the boy's scorn. He could almost hear the words the boy might say - the words that had played over and over in his head for the last eighteen years. "I ended up alone. You couldn't protect me, and you won't be able to protect her. You'll fail her too."

But he was determined not to. He wasn't sure what it was about Kenzi, but something about her made him want to break free, made him want to try again. Perhaps it was the simple way she seemed to accept him just the way it was. Perhaps it was her faith in God. Perhaps it was just the brilliant smile that warmed his soul when she flashed it his direction. Whatever it was, she was the first woman to pierce his wall in years, and he wasn't ready to give up. Not yet.

With a final sigh, he stepped out of his Mustang and headed toward the front door of the center. A small jingling sound announced his arrival, and Shelby glanced up with a smile.

"Hey, Blaine, Kenzi's not here if you were looking for her."

He wondered if Kenzi had told Shelby about their dates. Probably. Though his experience with women was limited, he'd heard the other guys talk enough to know that women loved to share those kind of experiences. Besides,

Shelby was looking at him differently, with a mischievous twinkle in her eye.

He shoved his hands in his jean pockets and rocked back on his heels. "I'm actually not here for Kenzi. I'm here because it's my day to hang out with the kids."

Shelby's eyes widened, and her mouth formed a silent "o". "Right, of course. I knew that." But the pink color spreading across her cheeks told him she had forgotten. Her head dropped to the counter in front of her as her hands sifted through the papers. "I just need to find your original form. Aha, here it is."

She brandished a piece of paper as if it were some lost treasure and then slid it across to him. "I just need you to check the information and make sure it's still accurate, so that we have it on file. Then you can add today to the bottom."

Blaine scanned the form, but everything appeared in order. He took the pen she handed him and began filling out the requested information.

"I'm actually really glad you came in today," Shelby continued, "I was going to ask Tucker if he could set up a time for me to come talk to the team or at least you anyway."

"What for?" he asked without looking up.

"I thought it would be a great idea if we started a Big Brother type thing here."

Blaine's grip on the pen increased, and a hole formed

in the paper from the pressure he was applying. A Big Brother program was out of the question. At least for him. It would involve taking the child out of the center and being responsible for them, and there was no way he was doing that. No way.

"The guys on the team could each adopt one of the kids here as a younger brother or sister. Take them out, hang out with them, with parental permission of course."

"No." The word came out more forcefully than he intended and cut off Shelby's explanation.

Her mouth hung open as she stared at him. "No? Why not? The kids would love it."

Great. Now, he'd done it. How did he convince her not to do this without telling her his real reason? "I just... We're going to be too busy with the season starting soon. Maybe that's an idea we can save for after the season ends."

She stared at him, and he knew she was trying to decide if he was telling the truth. No doubt she would ask Tucker to confirm Blaine's excuse. Should he try to convince Tucker to agree with him? He had a feeling that Tucker wouldn't lie for him. He'd changed since becoming a believer. Would the man agree on his own? It was possible. The schedule was challenging, especially at the beginning of the season, but Tucker might think helping the kids was more important than their challenging season.

"Okay, I'll table the idea for now," her voice held a

note of sadness, "I still think it's a good one."

Blaine breathed a sigh of relief. It wasn't a perfect solution, but it was better than nothing, and maybe by then he would be able to take it on. "So, what would you like me to do today?"

"The kids really love when you guys teach them drills or whatever it is you do for football. Do you have some you could share?"

Blaine smiled at Shelby's clear lack of knowledge about the sport. He'd have to remember to tease Tucker about it later. If he was planning to marry this woman, she needed to at least have a working idea of the game. "I can probably figure something out."

"Great. Two of our high schoolers are with them now, but I'm sure they'd love a break."

Blaine nodded and continued into the main gym area. The kids were playing some form of tag with two teenagers, but the game came to a screeching halt when they saw him. Almost like a tidal wave, they discarded their game and came barreling toward him.

He recognized many of the faces from the Christmas party and the last few times he had volunteered, but there were several new ones as well. Word must be spreading and the thought made him smile. Kids needed a place like this.

"You're Blaine Hollis, aren't you?" The question came from one of the newer faces, a stocky boy who had all the classic markings of a bully - the fierce eyes, the crossed arms, the tight line of his lips.

"I am. How would you guys like to learn how to throw a football today?" Blaine quickly scanned the room. He knew the center had used some of the money they'd received to buy new footballs, but he wasn't sure if they would have enough for all the kids. They'd have to take turns.

"I want to learn how to throw a football," a young girl with braids piped up.

The bully turned on her. "Girls don't play football. They can't throw and they definitely can't take a hit."

The girl's face fell, and her head dropped to her chest. Blaine knew he should do something, say something, but was he allowed?

"That's not true. Girls can play football if they want to." He saw the girl look up at him. "There are a lot of people in this world who will try to tell you what you can't do, but the only one who really knows that is you." He shot a pointed stare at the bully before turning back to the girl. 'What's your name?"

"Belinda." Her voice was quiet as if she wasn't sure she believed him, and he noticed her eyes shift to gage the other boy's reaction.

"Well, Belinda, how would you like to be my helper today? I'll show you first and when you have it down, you can help me show the other kids. Would you like that?"

The light returned to her eyes and her shoulders lifted a little higher. "I'd like that."

He held out his hand to her and let her lead the way to the sports closet.

KENZI

Kenzi smiled as she responded to the text from Blaine. He was off tomorrow and willing to meet her at the cabin to remove the old furniture if it worked for her schedule. She had nothing pressing taking priority over his job, so she'd readily agreed. Besides, she couldn't wait to see him again.

He hadn't kissed her the other night, even after dinner, but she'd seen the want in his eyes more than once, and the want was definitely in her eyes. She'd been thinking about his lips a lot lately. A lot. Perhaps tomorrow at the cabin would be the perfect opportunity, but before she let her mind skip too far down that trail, she needed to let Shelby know the good news.

The venue she had wanted for the wedding, an old church with an elaborate reception area, had just responded to Kenzi's message that they were available. Even though the wedding was still months away, Kenzi knew she would need to devote a lot of her time to making it the perfect space for Shelby, especially after she finished Blaine's cabin. Hopefully, by then she would have some more jobs lined up, but currently her phone was still silent. Though daunting, she was trying hard not to be discouraged. She knew that if worse came to worse, she could always return to the center and work with Shelby, but that wasn't what she wanted.

"God, I think decorating is my call, but I want to make sure I'm following Your will. Please show me if I'm wrong and open doors if I'm right." The short prayer was one she'd been repeating often, but she knew that God worked in His time and not in hers. "Oh, and please give me a sign about Blaine. I know something is going on with him, but I don't know how much I should invest. Can you help me guard my heart if he's not the guy for me?" Though she heard no audible reply, she knew He had heard her and would answer. As hard as it was, she would be patient.

Grabbing her laptop and purse from the passenger seat, Kenzi stepped out of the car and headed for the center. Shelby would probably just be closing, so it was a perfect time to meet her.

The front door was already locked, but thankfully Kenzi still had her key. She unlocked the door and called out, "I've got good news," before locking the door behind her again.

Shelby's head popped up in the reception window. She'd probably been running the reports for the night. "Oh yeah? I've got some news too, but you go first."

Kenzi continued around the small reception area to the open door and set her computer and purse on the table. "I got a call from the church you wanted. They can fit you in, so we need to decide how you want it to look."

"That is fantastic," Shelby said as she sat next to Kenzi, "but I'm not sure I have that all figured out yet. I know I want pink and white flowers and tulle and ribbons, but you are way better at what it will look like than I am."

"Okay, well that at least gives me some ideas to work with." Kenzi opened her laptop and pulled up a blank document to begin typing the notes in. "Do you care what kind of flowers?"

"Ranunculus. I've always loved how they looked, and maybe a few orchids. Only a few though for some color. I know they're expensive."

Kenzi noted the choices and tried to picture the flowers. If she was right, ranunculus looked similar to white roses only fuller. "Peonies might be pretty too, but they're also kind of pricey. Oh, and once I saw this bouquet that had flowers that trailed down like ribbons."

"Stephanotis," Shelby said with a nod. "Yeah, those are pretty and inexpensive."

Kenzi narrowed her eyes at her friend. "When did you get so informed on flowers' names?"

Pink spread across Shelby's cheeks along with a look of chagrin as if she'd been caught stealing cookies from the jar. "Since I got engaged. I've been spending my free time in the evenings going over pictures and finding what I liked. I figured I might as well learn their names too."

Kenzi wondered if she would be like that if she ever got engaged, and then she realized she'd probably be worse. The designer in her wouldn't allow anything mismatched or out of place. Her poor future husband. "Okay, well that sounds good. I can start working up some ideas based on this, and if you think of anything else you can always reach out to me. Now, what was your news?"

Shelby's smile faded and concern flooded her eyes. "Are you still working with Blaine?"

Uh oh. Shelby looked as if bad news was coming next. "Yeah, why?"

Shelby bit her bottom lip and stared at the table a moment before speaking again. "He came in today, for his day here. You know how they're doing one day a month?"

Kenzi nodded. She was aware of the plan. "Was he awful or something? I thought he did fine the last few times he was here." She knew she was falling for him, but if he wasn't good around children, would that change her opinion? She did want to be a mother one day.

"No, he was great with the kids. He stood up to one of our newer kids who's a bit of a bully and really made this little girl's day."

"But?" Kenzi didn't know why Shelby looked apprehensive. That was good news. She wished she'd had someone like Blaine to stand up for her in middle school when the bullying and teasing was the worst. She thought back to her last day of eighth grade.

Kenzi's stomach clenched as she watched Tyson James take the white board marker. The teacher had allowed the students to play Win, Lose, or Draw on the board, and Tyson had nearly bounded out of his seat to be the first. She wasn't sure what to make of Tyson. He always seemed to have a cruel word to throw her way as they passed in the hall, but he would always end it with a wink. Her mother had assured her that he was only picking on her because he liked her, but Kenzi wasn't so sure.

He began drawing across the white board, and her heart sank as she saw a stick figure come to life. Around her, the other kids began guessing, but Tyson just laughed and kept drawing. As soon as he added the pants, rounding around the waist, she knew he was drawing her. She'd put on a few pounds this year, but her mother had refused to purchase any more, claiming that Kenzi should just lose weight or take responsibility and buy her own clothes if she wanted more after the initial beginning of year purchase. Tyson hadn't let her too tight pants go unnoticed and often asked her if maybe she should consider skipping a few lunches.

As soon as he stepped back, one of his friends piped up. "It's Kenzi, getting ready for feeding time." Laughter broke out across the room, and Kenzi grabbed her bag and fled.

She'd spent the rest of the day in the nurse's office, hiding out. That event had been the straw that broke the camel's back and sent her on her strict journey of eating better and staying in shape. Even though she had entered high school looking completely different, that memory of eighth grade had stayed with her and affected her self-confidence. How different it might have been if one of her classmates had stood up for her.

"But... I floated an idea by him about the players being Big Brothers to the kids, and he was dead set against it."

"Did he say why?" Kenzi was still getting to know Blaine, but she couldn't see him not wanting to help out the kids, especially after the story Shelby had just shared.

"He said it was because the players would be too busy at the start of the season, but I don't think that was the real reason. I'm only saying something because I want you to be careful. I know you've had a crush on him for ages, and I was pushing you toward him at the dinner."

Kenzi placed a hand on Shelby's arm to stop her friend's rambling. "Don't worry. I am being careful. Something in his past is affecting him, but I don't know what yet. He told me something kept him from connecting emotionally but that he wanted to try with me."

An expression of deeper concern etched in Shelby's face, and she squeezed Kenzi's arm. "Just be careful. I don't want to see you get your heart broken."

Neither did Kenzi.

BLAINE

Blaine steeled himself for the onslaught of memories as he pulled up to the cabin. Though he still wasn't sure God would forgive him, he had been spending some time the last few days praying for the ability to get beyond his past. The blowup at Shelby had been a setback, but he was hopeful he would get through today without anything triggering him.

He turned off the engine and walked up the quiet path to the cabin. It was too bad it held such terrible memories for him because it really was a great space. A space to relax and unwind. Southlake wasn't a huge city, but it *was* still a city with noise and traffic and too many people. Sometimes, Blaine just wanted to get away.

He unlocked the front door and forced his feet over the threshold. When he'd been younger, he'd dreamed of the day the cabin would be his, when he could bring his wife and family here, but that had been before the accident. Now, just getting it sold and hoping some other family would find happiness here was enough for him.

Blaine shut the door behind him, and in the quiet, he could almost hear the sound of two boys running through the small floor plan. "We don't run in the cabin," their mother would say, and the echo of those words lingered in the air. But the boys would race up the stairs to the loft and grab their comic books and flashlights, or badger their parents to take them down to the lake. Those were always the best days, when their parents would take time off and let them swim in the lake.

The lake. The thought of it sent a shudder down his spine. He would not think about the lake now. Kenzi would be here soon and he needed to make sure he was in the right frame of mind to interact with her.

As if summoned by his thoughts, he heard the sound of a car pulling up to the cabin. He took a deep breath, pulled back his shoulders, and forced the unhappy memories from his mind.

"Sorry, I'm late," she said as she stepped out of her car. "Traffic was a bear leaving Southlake. You'd think there was a game going on or something." Her lips pulled into a small smile at her slight joke.

She looked different today, more relaxed. Her dark hair was pulled back into a ponytail, and her skirt had been traded in for a pair of comfy looking jeans. A short sleeve top was tied at the top of her jeans, displaying the tiniest line of skin, and his heart started in his chest. He liked her even more this way. Images of her wearing one of his jerseys and sitting in his box seat flashed through his mind, and he could see her fitting in with the other players' wives and girlfriends.

"No worries," he said, pushing that thought away. This was only their third date. He was a long way from proposals and wedding bells. "I just got here myself. Shall we get to work?"

She glanced around before shooting him a questioning look. "Where do you want to put everything? Just out here in the open?"

"Put everything?" And then it hit him. "I should have gotten a storage unit or something, right?"

Her lips mashed together, but he could tell she was holding back a smile. "Yeah, a storage container would have helped, but I brought some sanding supplies. We can start with the cabinets, and I'll see if I can get a storage unit out ASAP." She leaned back into the car and removed a box before shutting the door with her hip and continuing up the path. "I also have a plumber coming later to help remove the sink and the fridge, but I figured you and I could handle removing the cabinet doors and sanding and painting them. You don't mind getting a little dirty, do you?"

He laughed as he thought of how filthy he got in every game. He couldn't remember the last time a shower he'd taken after a game hadn't run brown for the first few minutes. "Until you've been tackled to the muddy ground by a three-hundred-pound linebacker, I don't think you even understand the meaning of dirty."

Her lips pulled into a wry smile as she eased past him and into the living room. "Touché, but I might be able to top that with cleaning vomit from the bathroom floor without a mop."

His face wrinkled in disgust. "Yuck, what did you clean it with?"

Kenzi rolled her eyes and laughed as she set the box down on the couch. "With a rag that I had to rinse in the sink repeatedly. It's a long story, but things have a tendency to get misplaced at the center if the kids get their hands on them. Let me tell you, that was not the day to lose the mop."

"Okay, yours might be grosser than mine." He couldn't believe they were actually comparing who had gotten dirtier. Kenzi was definitely different from any woman he'd gone out with lately.

"We'll see who takes the prize this afternoon." She held a screwdriver out to him and lifted her left eyebrow. "You know how to use this, right?"

He chuckled and nodded as he took it. Their fingertips brushed slightly, and he looked down at the heat burning up his hand. He was in so much trouble if just touching her fingertips did this to him.

Kenzi made a quick call on her phone for a storage unit, then grabbed a screwdriver from the box for herself before heading into the kitchen. He wouldn't have pegged her for being good with tools, but she kept up with his pace as they unscrewed all the cabinet doors and laid them on the table.

Half an hour later, his shoulders burned, but the adrenaline of hard work pumped through him. He enjoyed using his muscles, feeling them stretch and constrict. It was probably one reason he enjoyed football. It was a physical sport, and he was always exhausted when the game ended.

"Need a break?" Kenzi teased as he collapsed into one of the kitchen chairs.

The grueling work had caused a few strands of her hair to escape the ponytail's hold, and sweat now glued them to her forehead, but somehow it worked on her. He wondered if she had any idea how beautiful she was with her messed up hair and bright eyes.

"I'm fine," he said, answering her question. "Just a little thirsty."

"Allow me," she said, grabbing two cups out of the now-open cupboard and filling them with water. She handed one to him and took a long swig of hers. When it was empty, she set it on the counter and turned to him. "Ready to sand?"

He wasn't sure he was, but there was no way he was going to let her best him. "Bring it on," he said, setting his own cup down and picking up one of the doors. She walked into the living room and returned with a sander in each hand.

"Pick your poison."

The sanders looked exactly the same to him, but he took a second longer just to make sure before grabbing the one in her left hand. "Let's do this."

"Outside though," Kenzi said with a laugh. "I know we plan to redo the floors, but there's no reason to dirty it all up before then."

Blaine glanced out the back door. "Outside? You mean on the porch?" He'd been doing so well - ignoring the memories and pretending they didn't bother him - but could he really sit on the porch that close to the lake without his past overtaking him?

"Unless that's a problem." She raised an eyebrow at him as she waited for his answer.

He swallowed the lump that was threatening to choke off his air and pulled his shoulders back. He could do this. If he didn't look at the lake, if he sat with his back to it, then surely, he could do this. "No, it's fine."

KENZI

Kenzi tried to keep her focus on the task at hand, but Blaine and his muscular arms kept dragging her attention away from her door. He looked at home sanding doors, but then he had said he had some carpentry skills, so she shouldn't be surprised. Really, she was just glad to see him smiling. The last time they'd been at this cabin, he'd been different. Sullen. Like an invisible weight lay around his shoulders. But today, he seemed lighter. He had still hesitated about going outside, and he was sitting with his back to the lake, but it was an improvement from last time, and she was definitely enjoying the banter they were trading back and forth.

"Done," he said, laying his last door down. He looked at her stack, still three to go, and shook his head. "I thought you said you were good at this."

Some noise that was a cross between a snicker and a snort escaped her mouth. "I never said that. I just asked if you were ready." Ugh, why couldn't she scoff like a normal person?

He chuckled - probably at her - and leaned back in his chair. "I suppose I should have made sure you were ready then. Shall I help you out?"

"If you want." She could finish her doors without a problem, but allowing him to help her would give her the opportunity to watch him a little longer.

"Well, I can't just sit here and watch you work. That hardly seems fair." He leaned across and grabbed the next door off her stack. "I don't know if I ever asked you, and I know this is only your second job, but have you always been into design?"

Kenzi pursed her lips as she thought. "I guess in a way. I remember always wanting to change my room around. It drove my mother nuts. I would move my bed from one side of the room to the other." She chuckled at the memory of her frazzled mother banging her toe against something in Kenzi's room that hadn't been in that spot the day before. "She finally said I was only able to rearrange the furniture once a month and paint once a year. It was high school when I got into fashion. I suppose the two kind of work together, but it's not what I originally went to college for."

"No?" His eyebrow lifted on his head, but his focus remained on the door he was sanding.

"No. I thought I wanted to be an actress and then a lawyer and then a journalist." Kenzi couldn't believe how flighty she had been. "After a few years, I decided I didn't know what I wanted to do, but I should probably stop wasting my parent's money. So, I worked with Shelby for a while. Decorating for the Christmas party was my first gig, I guess you could say, though I didn't get paid for it. Still, I think I knew then that was where my passion lay."

"It's good to find your passion," he said with a nod. "It certainly makes a job seem less like work."

"Do you think carpentry is your passion? I mean when

you retire from football?" She knew he still had a few good years left, but few football players were still playing in their mid-thirties and even fewer quarterbacks. Shoulder injuries or concussions from all the hits tended to put them into retirement sooner.

His sanding paused for a moment as if he was contemplating her question. His jaw tightened, and his shoulders rose with a deep breath. Then the sanding resumed. "I don't know."

He'd paused for so long, she'd begun to wonder if he was going to answer the question, and she certainly hadn't expected what he had said. He seemed like someone who knew what he was doing with his life, but this, apparently, was one area he hadn't figured out completely. Nor did he appear to want to talk more about it. She wondered if it had anything to do with whatever had happened in his past. "Well, I'm sure whatever you decide to do, you'll be great at it. I haven't seen you be bad at anything yet."

She looked over to see him flash a half smile, but before either of them could say more, the sound of a large truck pulling up to the cabin carried on the air.

"Ooh, I think our storage container might be here."

BLAINE

Blaine couldn't believe the hideousness of the monstrosity the truck dropped off. The container was huge and grey and ugly. "This won't stay long, right?"

Kenzi rolled her eyes and shook her head. "No, just long enough for us to load up all the furniture and get the floors redone. Then, we'll move the stuff we're keeping back in, and this bad boy," she banged on the side sending a hollow metallic sound through the air, "will go away."

"Good. Let's get started." He wasn't sure what was bothering him so much about the storage container, but something about the sight of it just rubbed a nerve.

Kenzi nodded and led the way back into the cabin. "Let's load the furniture first, and then we can look at packing up some of the smaller items."

Hefting the two couches was not an easy feat, but Blaine was impressed that Kenzi held her own, and though beads of sweat broke out on her forehead and trickled down the side of her face, she did not give up.

He was able to grab the chair by himself, leaving her the coffee table. It wasn't extremely large, so he figured she could muscle it out herself. As he placed the chair in the container though, he realized Kenzi wasn't behind him. Had she had trouble with the table after all? Or had she tripped and injured herself? The thought spurred him into action, and he burst out of the container to scoop her up. But she was not on the ground. Nor was she injured inside the cabin.

Instead he found her rooted to the spot in the center of the room. The table was on its side as if she had lifted it and then had to set it back down, but that wasn't what held his attention. The faded piece of newspaper she held in her hand was what held his attention and hers too as she didn't even look up when he entered.

In fact, it wasn't until he was only a few feet from her that she seemed to realize he was there. Her eyes lifted to his, and they were filled with sadness. And he knew. He knew what the paper in her hand said. He knew she had read it, and he knew that she would never look at him the same way again. He'd seen the same sadness in everyone's eyes after the accident. It had been in his father's eyes when he told Blaine about the divorce and in his mother's eyes when she moved them from their house. He had never wanted to see it in Kenzi's eyes, and now it would always be there.

"Blaine..." It was all she could seem to manage. Emotion strangled her voice and pity flowed from her gaze.

"Don't," he said, snapping the paper from her. "Don't say you're sorry. Don't say it wasn't my fault." He could feel the anger boiling inside him. The red-hot anger he had buried for years and successfully kept down was now clawing up his throat and demanding to be let out.

"Is this why you've never had a relationship? Why you think you can't connect?"

She was probably asking out of curiosity and concern, but that didn't matter to Blaine. "I said don't. I don't want to talk about it. In fact, I don't think this was a good idea." His voice came out in a growl, much harsher than he meant it to be, but he seemed unable to tame the fire burning through him.

"This?" Confusion contorted her pretty features, and then her face shifted, hardened. "Do you mean me decorating the cabin? Or do you mean us?"

Blaine could hear the hurt in her voice, see it written all over her face, but he couldn't take back his words. He had known coming back here was a mistake. He should have forfeited the inheritance and let the lawyer deal with it or left the cabin the way it was and put it up for sale himself. Bringing Kenzi here had been a mistake and getting involved with her... His thought trailed off as his fists balled at his side. He had known better. "Maybe both."

He regretted the words as soon as he said them. They cut her in a way a knife never could. He saw her flinch, saw her jaw clench and her eyes tear up, and then he saw her grab her bag and walk out of the door and out of his life.

Blaine sank to the floor and stared at the faded newspaper story. Would he ever get past this?

KENZI

Tears blurred Kenzi's vision as she drove. She should have known better. No, she did know better. There was a reason her father always said to keep work and play separated, but how could she have known Blaine would blow up at her like that?

She'd had no idea what the paper was when it fluttered out of the table, and her heart had broken for Blaine as she read the story. No wonder he had trouble connecting emotionally. No wonder he hid behind so many walls, but why push her away now that she knew? That was what hurt the most. She'd thought they were building something, something they could share, but he'd only been pretending. Just like Brian. Just like Jeff. Why did she always seem to fall for guys who weren't able to commit?

Even worse, what was she going to do now? She'd have to give back the rest of the money Blaine had paid her. She couldn't keep it. And she had no other jobs lined up. The other jobs she had applied for still hadn't called. Maybe she didn't have what it took to be a designer. Maybe the job redoing the center had been offered out of pity from the team. They'd seen her as this pretty girl in her mid-twenties who hadn't known what she wanted out of life and they'd thrown her a bone. Maybe she was destined to go through life without a real talent, with only a pretty face. All the memories of middle school, junior high, and later of Jeff flooded her mind.

"Stop it," she said the words aloud as she banged on the steering wheel. "This is Blaine's issue. Not yours." The words were easy to say but a lot harder to believe. Ever since the incident with Brian and the teasing in junior high, her confidence had been shot.

Then, she'd reached high school and changed her image. She'd lost weight, discovered fashion, and met Jeff. And she'd thought Jeff really cared for her, but then he'd dumped her after homecoming and told her he'd only been seeing her to be assured the crown. Kenzi had told no one, not even Shelby. It had been too embarrassing, so instead, she'd put on a good front and claimed they had a fight. It had worked- on the outside - but inside, she was still that pre-teen girl looking for acceptance, for love, and not finding it.

She didn't even bother to warn Shelby she was coming. Kenzi knew she would be at home working on wedding plans. Her tears waited until she knocked on Shelby's door, but when the door opened and she saw the look of concern on her friend's face, she could hold them back no longer.

"What's wrong?" Shelby led her inside and to the couch.

Kenzi shook her head as the tears flowed down her face. She couldn't form words just yet. Emotions clenched her throat, blocking any sound other than sobs. Shelby placed her arm around Kenzi and let her cry. She seemed to know that's what she needed most.

When the tears finally slowed and her throat loosened up, Kenzi lifted her head to look at Shelby. "I think I just got fired."

Shelby's eyes widened. "What? You must be mistaken. Surely he didn't fire you."

Kenzi shook her head. "He told me he didn't think it was a good idea. I asked him if he meant hiring me or dating me and he said both."

Confusion covered Shelby's face. "That makes no sense. I thought things were going well."

"They were and then I found something I don't think I was supposed to see. We were moving furniture out in order to take out the old flooring, and when I picked up a table, a newspaper clipping fell out. I didn't know what it was or I never would have read it."

"I don't understand. What was in the newspaper clipping?"

Kenzi took a deep, shuddering breath. "The death of his brother."

❧ 14 ❧

BLAINE

Anger still floated around Blaine as he pulled into the training facility Monday morning. After he'd sent Kenzi away, he'd not only had to finish taking out the furniture by himself, but he'd had to deal with the plumber and the flooring guy. Neither of them would be singing his praises to anyone soon. In addition, guilt over how he'd treated Kenzi had plagued him the rest of the weekend. He knew she didn't deserve the way he'd yelled at her, and now he had no idea how to make it right.

Even though breakfast was the first thing on the agenda, Blaine walked to the locker room before heading to the cafeteria. He hoped a few minutes of silence and solitude would calm him enough that he could face his teammates without displaying his anger. He'd certainly told them often enough not to bring emotions into the practices. Unfortunately, his hope for solitude was whisked away at the sight of Tucker in the room.

Tucker glanced up, and his stance stiffened when he saw Blaine. "You told Shelby we couldn't do the big brother thing? Why?"

Blaine sighed as he set his bag down. He'd been hoping Shelby wouldn't mention the issue to Tucker, but he should have known better. "I have my reasons, but mainly because the season starts next week. We need our focus to be on the game. Teams are going to be gunning for us this year after our championship win last year, and we can't get distracted by outside influences."

Tucker folded his arms across his chest and raised his eyebrows. "Outside influences like Kenzi?"

Okay, Tucker had him there. He should have chosen his words better. "Kenzi is helping me redecorate a cabin I inherited so I can sell it." Was she still helping him? He was no longer sure.

"That's not the entire truth, and you know it." Tucker shook his head. "You may have hired her, but you were also dating her. You can't lie to me, man. Not when I'm engaged to her best friend."

"We went on three dates," Blaine said as he shoved his bag into his locker. "I'd hardly call that dating."

"Don't do that to her."

"Do what?" Blaine asked, but he knew the answer.

"Don't treat her like the other women that you go out with once or twice and then dump. I know something happened between the two of you the other day. Shelby told me Kenzi showed up at her place and was a mess. Now, I know you're the captain, but something is going on with you, Blaine, and it's not good. You told me once that I needed to change my perspective. Well, I don't know what your deal is, but maybe it's time you change your perspective. Those kids need us. They look up to us, and all Shelby is asking is that we take some time and hang out with them. I don't think that's too much to ask, even during our season."

"I can't be a big brother." The words exploded out of Blaine's mouth and reverberated in the locker room, but he was almost glad. This secret had been tearing him up for years, and saying the words out loud brought a small sense of relief.

Tucker threw his hands out in exasperation. "Why not? It's just spending some time with someone younger. Take them out to movies, the park. What's so hard about that?"

"Because I was a big brother once, and I let my little brother drown." Blaine collapsed onto the bench and hung his head. "I couldn't protect him, and I can't be responsible for another kid."

Tucker sat down next to him and placed a hand on his shoulder. "Blaine, I'm sure whatever happened wasn't your fault."

"No, it was my fault. We were supposed to be reading in the cabin, but I got bored. I suggested we go out on the lake even though my parents said we weren't to go outside. He trusted me, so he went with me." Blaine rubbed a hand across the back of his neck as the memories rushed in.

"At first it was great. The lake had frozen over and we were sliding all over the place. Then I heard the crack and Kevin's scream. I saw him go down, but I couldn't swim and neither could he." He closed his eyes and shuddered as the hardest memory of all surfaced in his mind's eye. "I could see him under the ice, but I couldn't get to him. I watched him drown."

There was a moment of silence before Tucker let out a long sigh. "Okay, that's definitely a heavy weight to bear, but you were just a kid, Blaine. You should never have been put in that situation, but I think you've carried this long enough."

Blaine's head shot up. "How can you say that? He was my brother!"

"I know, but what happened was an accident. You remember how angry I was last year?"

Blaine nodded, wondering what this had to do with his story.

"Well, my mother died when I was young. Then, my father grew distant and threw himself into his work. I thought he blamed me for my mother's death somehow, but really he was just grieving."

"I'm sorry for your loss, Tucker, but what does that have to do with me?"

Tucker's lips pulled into small smile. "I'm telling you because you saw what the misconception did to me. I turned to anger and drinking. You've distanced yourself from people, but you deserve love, Blaine. You deserve a relationship, and I don't know if Kenzi is that girl for you, but don't you think you owe it a chance?"

Blaine looked at his friend and wondered if he was right. Maybe it was time he changed his perspective.

KENZI

The knock on the door startled Kenzi out of her daydream. Or nightmare more like it. The bills were coming due, and now she had no money and no job on the horizon. She couldn't believe how things had turned bad so quickly.

She closed her laptop as she pushed back from the table. A hand-me-down from her mother, it was still in pristine condition as was everything her parents owned. Even though it belonged to Kenzi now, she still had trouble putting a glass down without a coaster or doing any design work at it in case her pen slipped and marred the tabletop. Her mother believed that people judged you by your house, and that had been drilled into Kenzi.

She glanced at her watch as she crossed to the front door. It was nearly eight. Other than Shelby, she knew of no one who would show up at her door so late. Her parents certainly wouldn't, and she didn't have many other close friends. She hoped Tucker and Shelby hadn't had a fight. There was no doubt they would one day, but so far, they'd been like two people sharing one mind.

Her heart tightened as she peeked through the spy hole to see Blaine Hollis standing on her doorstep. His hands were shoved in his jean pockets, but his face was impossible to read. She bit her lip as she unlocked the door. If he was here to demand his money back, she didn't know what she would do. She'd used most of it to purchase the floors and hire the plumber.

When the door opened and she saw his face up close, that thought flew from her head. His shoulders were rolled forward, and a look of contrition covered his face. "Hey, Kenzi, can I come in?"

She stepped back, allowing him entrance. She had no idea why he was here, but something was definitely weighing on him. "Would you like to sit down?" Her hand pointed to the couch, but it was more out of habit than an actual request.

His eyes darted around the room before he shook his head. "No, I'll be quick. I came to say I'm sorry."

She waited to see if he would expound. What exactly

was he sorry for? Hiring her? Asking her to dinner? Yelling at her?

"I don't know if you read the whole story on that newspaper clipping, but I lost my little brother when I was ten. He was my best friend. My parents trusted me to watch him inside, but I got bored and convinced him to go out on the lake with me." He lifted one hand from his pocket and ran it across the back of his neck.

"It had been cold that winter, and the lake had frozen. I didn't know the ice wasn't thick enough to hold us. When Kevin went under, I tried to save him, but neither of us could swim, and I couldn't get him back to the part where he'd fallen in.

Kenzi gasped and covered her gaping mouth with her hand. The newspaper certainly hadn't shared that bit of information in its story.

"My life fell apart after that. My parents got divorced. My dad turned to drinking, and my mom worked two jobs just to keep us in a tiny apartment. I lost my brother and my family that winter, and I don't have relationships because I don't want to fail anyone else. Nor am I sure I could handle the pain of losing anyone else, but I shouldn't have taken it out on you." He shook his head and took a few steps away from her.

"I felt different with you, but then you found the story, and I knew you would look at me differently. Everyone looks at me differently when they find out." He paused as if waiting for her to say something. Then he shrugged. "Anyway, I'm sorry."

Kenzi felt the weight of his guilt, and she placed a hand on his arm. "Blaine, you were just a kid. I'm sorry about your brother, but you've beat yourself up long enough. It's time to forgive yourself."

"How am I supposed to do that?"

"With God's help."

Blaine lifted his arm to run his hand across the back of his neck. "I don't think God wants anything to do with me."

"That's where you're wrong, Blaine. God loves you. He sent His son to die for you. For all of us. It sounds awful, but the death of your brother was not a surprise to Him. Nor is what you're feeling now, but that doesn't mean He loves you any less."

Blaine's hand shifted to his chin. "Do you really believe that?"

Kenzie crossed to him and placed a hand on his arm. "I do, and if you'll let me, I'd love to help you know Him like I do."

He held her gaze, and she could feel the emotions flowing between them. They crackled like electricity in the air.

"I'd like that." His voice was husky, and his eyes shifted from hers down to her lips and back again. He wanted to kiss her, and she wanted that too, more than anything.

Her hand found his chest, and she could feel his heart-beat pounding beneath her palm. She lifted her face to his, and before she could move another inch, his mouth was on hers. Tentative at first, his lips barely brushed against hers, soft as a whisper. Was he afraid she would say no?

She moved her hands to behind his neck and stood on her tiptoes in order to deepen the kiss. And boy did it work. Her knees trembled and grew weak, and though she knew there was nothing there, she could have sworn she heard the sound of explosions. She had never experienced a kiss like that in her life, and he responded as if she were a lifeline in the ocean. His lips explored hers as if they held the answer to relieve his pain.

"Does this mean I'm not fired," she asked when they finally pulled back.

Blaine laughed and responded with another kiss. "You're definitely re-hired, and I may just owe you a bonus for putting up with me."

Kenzi knew there was a serious truth to his lighthearted words, but she had already fallen for Blaine. She just hoped he wouldn't break her heart.

❦ 15 ❦

BLAINE

Blaine took a deep breath before entering the center. After his conversation with Kenzi last night, he knew he needed to apologize to Shelby. He was still terrified to be alone with a kid, but he hoped with her help that he could move past that.

"Blaine, what are you doing here?" Shelby looked at him and then down to a clipboard. "I didn't know you were on the schedule today."

"I'm not. I came to apologize to you for my behavior the other day."

A look of confusion crossed her face for a moment, and then her eyes widened. "About the Big Brother thing."

"Yeah, I wasn't completely honest with you. Our schedule *is* about to get busy, but I said no because I was afraid. My brother died when I was supposed to be watching him, and I was afraid the same thing might happen to one of these kids if they were left in my care. To be honest, I still am afraid. However, Kenzi and Tucker have promised to help me, and these kids do deserve it. It's a great idea, Shelby."

Shelby's eyes were an ocean of compassion. "Blaine, I'm so sorry to hear about your brother, but thank you for telling me. We'll set it up so that you feel comfortable, whether that means having your time here or making sure someone else is always with you, we'll make it work."

"Thank you."

As Blaine left the center, he felt a little lighter. He'd been carrying around this weight by himself for so long that it felt good to share it with others, even if all they could do was lend a listening ear.

Climbing into his Mustang, he pointed the car toward the lake house. Since it was his day off from training, he and Kenzi had made plans to meet up and put the doors back on in the kitchen.

The large storage container was still outside the cabin when he pulled up as was Kenzi's car. She had said she wanted to get an early start to check the floor installation. Blaine had left the cabin unlocked for the flooring guy before he left for the weekend because the man had said it would take a few days to finish the job.

His mouth dropped open in surprise when he opened the front door moments later. The room not only looked different without the old furniture, but now a beautiful hardwood floor covered the floor. He'd agreed to let Kenzi change the floor because he figured it would raise the value of the cabin, but now he could see what she had seen in her head. It made all the difference in the world. The grain in the floor complemented the exposed wood in the living room, and even without furniture, the place felt warm and inviting.

Kenzi appeared in the doorway that led to the kitchen. "It's nice, right?"

"It's more than nice. It's amazing. You have a real knack for this, Kenzi."

A soft blush colored her cheeks, and her teeth chewed at her bottom lip. "Thank you, but I still haven't lined up another job after this one. It doesn't matter how great I am if I can't get people to take a chance on me."

He entered the rest of the way and closed the door behind him. "You let me worry about that. I've got an idea that should have your phone ringing off the walls soon."

She raised her eyebrow in silent question, but he wasn't prepared to share that secret yet. "Trust me. It will be great. Now, how about we finish those doors?"

"I thought you'd never ask." She held a screwdriver out to him, and he laughed as he joined her in the kitchen.

She turned some music on with her phone and Blaine chuckled as she bopped to the beat while screwing the doors back on. When the song shifted and slowed, he dropped his screwdriver and grabbed her hand, pulling her to his chest for an impromptu dance.

"I know it's short notice, Kenzi, but our first game is Sunday, and I'd love to have you in the box seat cheering me on. Do you think you can make it?" His heart paused as he waited for her answer. Asking her was a huge step for him. He'd never asked a woman to use his tickets before; he'd never wanted the media to associate him with any of them, but he didn't mind being seen with Kenzi.

She tilted her head and stared thoughtfully at him as her hand caressed the back of his neck. "I will; on one condition."

"Condition?" His throat constricted at the word. Was she going to ask him to face his fear? Or talk about his brother? He was glad that she knew, but he wasn't sure he was ready to share any more just yet.

"Don't worry. It's nothing too bad." She smiled up at him. "I want you to come to church with me tomorrow night. I know you can't do Sunday due to the game, but we have a great sermon on Wednesday night too, and I think you really need God back in your life to heal completely."

His jaw tightened as he swallowed. She was probably right, and he'd seen the change God had made in Tucker's life. But was he really ready for that? Was he ready to forgive God for taking his brother? Was he ready to trust that God would forgive him? He took a deep breath and nodded. "Okay. I will."

The happiness that radiated from Kenzi told him he'd made the right choice even though his stomach still clenched at the thought.

KENZI

Kenzi walked to her car on cloud nine that evening. Not only had she spent an amazing afternoon with Blaine, but he'd said yes. He'd asked her to come to his game on Sunday which was exciting, but more importantly he'd said he would go to church with her. She couldn't remember the last time a man had come to church with her. For that matter, she couldn't remember the last time she *wanted* a man to come to church with her. She had to tell Shelby.

Fishing her phone from her pocket, she set it up for hands free and then punched in her friend's number as she started the car. Shelby picked up on the third ring.

"He said yes," Kenzi said before her friend even had a chance to say hello.

Shelby laughed on the other end. "Well, hello to you too, Kenzi. Now please explain. Who said yes?"

"Blaine. He said he'd come to church with me tomorrow." She craned her head both directions as she exited Lost Lake Road. It hardly saw any traffic, but the street it connected with was a busy two-lane highway.

"That's great, Kenzi. I'm so glad."

"It was great. He loved the floors, and we got the cabinets up. He even danced with me in the kitchen. The cabin is actually coming along nicely, and he asked me to Sunday's game. Please tell me you're going too." She would go regardless, but she knew she would have much more fun with Shelby by her side.

"Yes, I'm going," Shelby said with a chuckle. "I think it's kind of expected now that we're engaged."

"Good. I can't believe this is happening, and I can't believe he said he'd come to church." Kenzi felt like a giddy school girl, like the way she had when Jeff Carpenter asked her to homecoming. Jeff Carpenter. The image of the broad-shouldered jock forced its way into her mind.

"Kenzi Lanham, how are you?"

Kenzi nearly dropped her books. Jeff Carpenter, starting quarterback for the football team, leaned against the locker next to hers. Even though he'd said her name, she still looked around as if unsure he meant to address her. "Me? You're talking to me?"

Her popularity had been increasing the last few years, ever since her fashion style began trending, but while she was enjoying attending parties and being greeted in the halls, Jeff Carpenter had never spoken to her until now. Was it because she'd finally made it on the cheerleading squad?

"Of course I'm talking to you. Homecoming is just around the corner, and I need to ask the prettiest girl in the school to be my date."

Kenzi blinked. She couldn't be the prettiest girl. She was still the chunky middle schooler in her head.

Jeff reached out and tucked a strand of hair behind her ear. "Say you'll go with me. I'd really like to get to know you better."

A horn blared, and Kenzi shook her head to clear the image from the past. She raised her hand in apology as the driver behind her sped past.

"Kenzi, you okay?" Concern filled Shelby's voice.

"Yeah, sorry, I spaced out for a second and a car honked at me. Shelby, what if he's like Jeff?"

"Jeff? Jeff who?"

"Jeff Carpenter from high school. You know the quarterback I dated for a few months. The one who..." She stopped herself from finishing the sentence.

"The one who broke your heart? Kenzi, why would you think he's like Jeff? Jeff was a jerk."

Kenzi bit her lip. She'd never told Shelby the whole story behind Jeff, but maybe it was time to now. Perhaps Blaine wasn't the only one who needed God's healing. She took a deep breath and let the story flow from her lips. "Shelby, Jeff and I didn't just break up. He dumped me after we were crowned and told me he'd only dated me to guarantee he would get the crown."

The sharp intake of breath belayed Shelby's shock. "I knew he was awful, but I had no idea. I'm so sorry, Kenzi."

Kenzi bit the inside of her lip. "Jeff's dumping me is part of the reason I've avoided relationships. I know Blaine isn't Jeff, but there are some similarities. I don't know if I could take it if he is playing with my emotions."

"Kenzi, Blaine has his own issues, but the nice part about them is that he knows better than to play with someone's emotions. If he asked you to the game and agreed to go to church, I think he meant it."

"You're right." Kenzi let out a shaky breath. "I've been guarding my heart, well trying to, since I knew his relationship with God was rather rocky, but maybe this is a sign of good things to come."

"Oh, Kenzi, I hope so. I've been praying for you guys, and I know Tucker has too."

"Thanks, Shelby. I'll see you tomorrow." As she hung up the phone, Kenzi knew she had some work to do on herself as well.

❄ 16 ❄

BLAINE

laine tugged at his collar as they approached the door of the large building. He hadn't been in a church in years, and while he didn't think he would be struck down by lightning or anything, he still worried that God might not want him back.

"Relax," Kenzi said, taking his hand. "I'm right here with you, and Shelby and Tucker will be here too."

The thought eased his anxiety slightly, and he forced his lips into a tight smile. He could do this. It wasn't a game, it wasn't taking care of a kid, it was just sitting through a sermon. An hour of his life, and maybe he could find the healing Kenzi hoped for.

Tucker and Shelby were already inside, and they greeted the two of them with wide smiles.

"Glad to see you could make it man," Tucker said, extending his hand as the two women hugged.

"Yeah, me too." Blaine shook Tucker's hand and hoped his teammate couldn't see how nervous he was.

"Don't worry. It'll be great. Coming back is hard, but life looks so much better when you do."

Blaine wasn't sure about that. Tucker's past had been hard but not as hard as Blaine's. Still, he was willing to enter with an open mind. Kenzi took his hand once again, and the four of them entered the large sanctuary.

Blaine wasn't sure he'd ever attended a Wednesday night service, and he was not prepared for the upbeat contemporary feel. Church had always been boring and a chore when he'd attended in his youth, but right now, with a full band on stage, it almost felt more like a concert. He found himself clapping to the beat and sharing a smile with Kenzi even though he didn't know the words to many of the songs.

When the music ended, a young man took the stage. He didn't appear to be much older than Blaine - no more than thirty for sure. Could pastors be that young?

"Good evening, everyone. I hope you are all having a blessed week. I feel like God has asked me to remind you of the story of Paul, and how it's never too late to come home."

Blaine's ears perked up as the man continued.

"I've had a lot of people tell me that they think God

won't accept them because they've done bad things, but we all know Paul was a disciple. Jesus picked him. What we forget sometimes is that Paul, before he found God, was one of the worst. Here was a man who condemned and killed Christians. He murdered the very people God loved, yet God still loved him and used him. Paul is an example for all of us. No matter what we've done or maybe haven't done, God still has a plan for us. He still loves us and seeks after us. All we have to do is open our hearts to Him and let Him work."

The pastor spoke longer, but Blaine didn't hear the rest. He was focused on the last few words. *All we have to do is open our hearts and let Him work.* His heart had certainly been closed for a long time. Was it really that easy?

Before he even knew what he was doing, he found himself whispering, "Please open my heart, Lord. Let me see You again."

Kenzi placed a hand on his knee and squeezed, and he wondered if she had heard his words. He decided it didn't matter. She was the reason his heart had thawed enough to be here, to hear this message. It was still too early to be certain, but he felt that Kenzi would be in his life for the foreseeable future.

KENZI

Kenzi replayed the night in her head as she brushed her teeth and got ready for bed. She was sure another piece of Blaine's emotional wall had fallen tonight. Near the end, she'd heard him whisper something though she couldn't make it out. She'd squeezed his knee to let him know she was there for him though.

The story had touched her too. While she hadn't been like Paul in the way the pastor spoke of, she knew her self-confidence issue was just as upsetting to God. He'd made her perfect, yet she couldn't see it. She'd felt that God grieved for her just as much as he did for Blaine. Just as much as he had for Paul, and as she'd listened to the sermon, she was reminded that she shouldn't care how others saw her because God saw her differently.

It was one thing to know it, but it sure was much harder to believe it. Especially when she'd checked her email upon arriving home to find that all the jobs she had applied for had turned her down. What was she going to do when she was done with Blaine's cabin? She had no second job lined up. Nor did she know how to go about drumming up business. She'd thought God was leading her into design, but maybe she'd been wrong again.

She turned out her bathroom light and padded to her bed. Perhaps if she spent some time alone with God, He might make the answer clear to her.

After situating herself on her bed with her legs crossed beneath her, she grabbed her Bible and opened it to the last book she'd been reading. Philippians was a pretty hopeful book anyway, but as she began reading chapter four, she marveled at how God could put the exact verse she needed in front of her. Worry about nothing, pray for everything, and thank Him for all He has done. Then peace will transcend. She definitely needed to do a little more of that.

She finished the chapter and then set her Bible aside. "God, thank you for the opportunity to work with Blaine. Thank you for bringing him into my life and for helping him open up about his past. Lord, if it's Your will, help us to grow stronger in You, and help me not to worry but know that You will provide the work I need. Amen."

The words didn't ease all of her anxiety, but she did feel a little better as she turned out the light and pulled the covers up over her shoulder.

Blaine couldn't keep his gaze from traveling up to the boxed seats as he threw the ball to Mason. Kenzi was up there with Shelby though he couldn't see her face, and it was the first time he'd had a woman in there cheering for him.

"What's the distraction, man?" Mason called out as he tossed the ball back. "That's the second pass you've thrown over my head."

Blaine pulled his attention from the glass windows just in time to catch the ball. "I'm sorry, Mason."

"It's a girl, isn't it?"

Blaine glanced quickly over at Tucker who was running sprints. "Did Tucker tell you?"

Mason laughed and caught the next pass easily. "He didn't have to. You've been happier than normal, and your gaze keeps traveling up to the box. I know what having a woman does to you."

His jaw tightened as he said the last words and Blaine could tell some woman had done a number on Mason in the past. Was that what his behavior at Christmas had been all about? He'd have to remind himself to check in with Mason later, when the first game of the season wasn't looming over their heads.

"You're right. It's a woman. I've never invited one before and I just keep wondering what she's thinking." He caught the ball, spun it in his fingers, and sent it sailing back.

"She's probably taking in the sites and enjoying the free food and being hounded by the other women," Mason said with a smile. "But if you keep getting distracted, then she's going to be worrying about you and your health when you keep getting sacked, so get your head in the game."

Blaine knew Mason was right. He spared one more glance at the box and then focused his attention on the warm-up. It was less than an hour to kickoff, and he needed to be prepared.

KENZI

Kenzi was glad Shelby was with her as they entered

the box. It wasn't her first time - she'd come to their Christmas game with Shelby last year - but it was her first time being here as Blaine's girlfriend. She wondered if the other women knew, if they would welcome her like they had Shelby.

"Don't worry," Shelby whispered in her ear as they made their way to the front chairs. "You've got this. Miss Southlake, remember?"

Kenzi managed a tight smile. Yes, she could put up a fake facade with the best of them - smile, wave, and pretend to be happy - but she wanted to be genuine with these women. If things worked out with Blaine, she'd be spending more time with them, and she wanted them to know the real her. Even if it meant sharing her faults.

"Shelby, so good to see you again."

Kenzi turned to the woman with the velvety voice and froze. It was Margaret, the owner's wife. She was a frightening woman. Not only did she ooze money on the outside, but she had a nasty habit of talking about the other women behind their backs. Kenzi had only heard a few of her comments at the Christmas game, but it was enough to let her know she wanted to avoid this woman as much as possible.

"Hello, Margaret. So good to see you again." Shelby's voice sounded just as bright as always, but Kenzi could see the stiffness in her posture. Evidently Shelby felt the same way toward Margaret as Kenzi did.

Margaret's icy blue eyes turned to Kenzi. "And who is your friend? I'm not sure we've met." The woman's gaze traveled up and down Kenzi, making her feel as if she were an item at an auction.

"This is Kenzi, my best friend and Blaine's girlfriend."

Margaret's eyes widened. "Girlfriend? I wasn't aware he had one."

Kenzi felt as if Margaret was examining her under a microscope. "I don't know if I'd say girlfriend, but he did invite me."

That was the wrong thing to say. Margaret's brow arched almost to her hairline. "So, you're not his girl-friend? Are you the flavor of the month then?"

The woman's harsh words and disdainful tone trans-ported Kenzi back to middle school. Embarrassment clawed at her face, and she stuttered as she tried to remedy her words. "I mean I don't know what we are yet. We've been on a few dates, but we haven't labeled our relation-ship yet."

"I see. Well, we'll see how long you last."

With that the woman spun away from them and toward her next victim. Kenzi sank down into the nearest chair and sighed. "That was awful."

"She's awful," Shelby said, sitting beside her and placing a hand on her arm. "Don't worry about her. Blaine wouldn't have asked you here if he didn't want you here.

Plus, he did come to church. I think things are going well for you guys."

Kenzi took a deep, shaky breath. "Yeah, you're right. I'm trying to work on not caring what people think, but it's hard, especially with a woman like her." She chanced a glance over her shoulder, but Margaret was engaged in a conversation with another woman.

"Maybe the game will take your mind off it," Shelby said softly.

The game. Right. Kenzi turned her attention back to the field and tried to enjoy the game.

K enzi looked down at the frame in her hands. She hoped Blaine would like it. It was the final piece to place in the cabin before she called it done and showed it to him.

The last few weeks had flown by for Kenzi. She'd spent nearly every day working at the cabin to finish it. The new appliances had arrived and been installed as had the beautiful new kitchen counter. Pillows and bedding and other accents had been purchased and placed artfully around the rooms. Even the bathroom vanity had made it in, though she'd worried about that one with Blaine's work schedule. Now that games had started, he was definitely busier than he had been before. When he wasn't at work, he was usually at home sleeping the exhaustion away. Still, he'd managed to find time to finish it as well as attend church with her when he was free.

She wasn't sure if he'd forgiven himself yet or come back to God completely, but he did appear to be improving. He could talk about Kevin without shutting down which was why she hoped he would appreciate the gift. She'd found an old picture of the two of them in the nightstand that had been upstairs and she'd had it blown up and framed. Kenzi hoped it might allow him to find peace and keep the cabin, but if not, then at least it would be something he could hang in his place.

"Knock, knock," he called as he stepped inside.

Kenzi tucked the frame she'd been holding behind her back and smiled as his eyes took in the place.

"Wow, this is amazing, Kenzi."

"Do you like it?" She knew it looked beautiful, but a part of her still needed to hear it from him.

"I do. It's," he paused and shook his head, "more than I ever thought it would be."

"Good." Her word came out in a sigh of relief. "I'll give you the tour in a minute, but I have one final touch that I wanted to add."

He tilted his head in question, and she smiled at him before walking over to the mantle and placing the framed picture on the top. She bit her lip and turned to face him, hoping she hadn't overstepped.

His jaw was tight - she could see it in the bulging vein

of his neck - but he didn't look angry. "Kenzi, this is…" His voice broke and he coughed to try and clear it. "Where did you find that?"

She stepped toward him. She ached to touch him, to make sure the shimmer she saw in his eyes was from happiness and not sadness, but she wanted to give him time to process. "I found the picture in the nightstand upstairs. I'm assuming that was where you and Kevin stayed when you were here."

He brought a fist to his mouth and nodded.

"I know this place has awful memories for you, Blaine, but I was hoping that maybe this would allow you to remember the good times too." She took another step and touched his arm.

His eyes found hers, and they were a hurricane of emotions. Had she made things worse? Then he pulled her into his arms and crushed her to his chest. "Thank you," he whispered into her hair. "Thank you."

BLAINE

Blaine took a deep breath and squeezed Kenzi's hand before pulling the door open. Today was the day he would meet his "little brother" or "little sister" and while he was feeling braver, especially with her by his side, his heart was still beating faster than normal.

"Hey guys," Shelby said as they approached the front desk.

"Hey, Shelby." He was glad to hear only a slight tremble in his voice. Kenzi flashed him a reassuring smile, and he soaked up the strength she sent his way.

"You ready to find out who your "little sister" is?"

A little sister. A sliver of relief coursed through him. It was still a small human being he was responsible for, but at least it wasn't a boy. Plus, Kenzi was here to help him. "Yes, I suppose I am." He smiled back at Kenzi.

"Great, because I have paired you with Darby. Her father was killed last year in the line of duty. She could really use a strong male presence in her life, and I thought you would be perfect."

Kenzi hugged his arm closer. "Darby is perfect. You'll love her."

He nodded as he tried to remember who Darby was. Generally, he was decent with names, but the added anxiety of working with kids had made it harder for him. He thought she was the cute girl with the big glasses, but he wasn't sure.

He and Kenzi continued into the gym and found Darby sitting with her mother at one of the makeshift tables that had been set up.

"Hello, Darby, I'm Blaine Hollis. Remember me?"

Darby looked up at him with her big brown eyes and nodded. "You're one of the football players, right?"

"That's right, I am, and if it's okay with you and your mom, I'm also going to be like your big brother."

"And big sister," Kenzi added. "You'll be our special sibling. Would you like that?"

Darby looked to her mother who smiled and nodded. Blaine could see the emotion building in her eyes.

"Will you do things with me like my dad did before he died?"

"We can do anything you want," Blaine said, squatting down so he was face to face with her. He was surprised at how easily the words came out of his mouth.

"My dad used to take me fishing. Will you take me fishing?"

Blaine paused as his heart stilled in his chest. Fishing meant water and water meant memories of Kevin sinking away from him forever. He couldn't do this. Shelby had made a terrible mistake; she'd have to find him another kid. He was about to say as much when he felt Kenzi's hand on his shoulder.

"You can do this." Her words were soft, barely more than a whisper, but the surety of them pushed a strength through him.

"I don't know much about fishing, but I can sure try. I don't have poles right now, but I'll get some." Darby's face fell in disappointment, so Blaine continued, "But it is a nice day out. Would you like to go to the lake and feed the ducks?"

Sunshine returned to Darby's face and a hopeful smile followed. She turned to her mother. "Can I?"

Her mother nodded and mouthed "thank you" to Blaine and Kenzi.

The look in the woman's eyes bolstered Blaine's courage even more. He could do this. She needed him to do this. Single motherhood was obviously wearing her down, and he could do this small piece to help her. Even if it meant being around water.

He took one of Darby's hands and Kenzi took the other. Together, they walked out of the center. As Darby swung their hands back and forth, he wondered seriously for the first time if he could have this someday. A wife. A kid. God was working on his heart, and he was falling for Kenzi, but he was still broken. Would she want a broken man?

After a quick stop at the store for some bread, he pulled into the parking lot of Southlake, the body of water for which the town was named. It wasn't a huge lake, but it was large enough that a path around the outside of it measured three miles from start to finish. It was nearly always bustling with activity from joggers, moms pushing strollers, and more. Today was no exception. Though it was nearing the end of October, the sun still shone brightly and it was warm enough to get by without a jacket.

After turning off the engine, he helped Darby out of the

seat, smiling as she bounced up and down on her feet. "Can I go feed them now?"

"Hold on, honey, we'll all go together," Kenzi said, as if she could sense Blaine's unease both with approaching the water and letting Darby go running off by herself.

His feet didn't start slowing until they were about ten feet from the water. Suddenly, it felt like he was walking in quicksand. His heart pounded in his ears and his throat dried up. He felt like a noose was slowly encircling his neck.

"Darby, honey, let's slow down for Blaine. Approaching the water is a hard thing for him."

Darby turned wide eyes up at him. "Why?" There was no condescension in her voice, just the curiosity of a child.

Blaine swallowed, knowing he had to answer her but unsure of how much to share. "I lost my brother when I was younger. He drowned."

Darby nodded as if this was the most natural thing in the world to hear. "I lost my dad recently so I know about being scared. But miss Kenzi and Miss Shelby told me that God was always holding my hand even when my daddy couldn't. Whenever I get scared, I just remember that." She squeezed his hand tighter. "I'll hold your hand like God does, so you'll understand, okay?"

Emotion overwhelmed Blaine, and he heard Kenzi sniffle beside him. How did this young girl have it all figured out when it had been years for him and he still struggled?

God, give me the faith of this child, he thought as he followed Darby closer to the lake's edge. A sense of peace covered him, and his heartbeat returned to normal. He opened the bag they had brought with them and handed a slice to Darby and one to Kenzi.

Darby smiled as she tore the bread and threw it out to the ducks who honked and fought for the pieces. Beside him, Kenzi nudged his shoulder and flashed him a smile. She was so amazing. He would have to do something in return for her. And he knew just what he could do.

❧ 19 ❧

BLAINE

Blaine opened the door to the cabin and smiled at the woman on the other side. "Diane, thanks for coming." Diane was a photographer for Novel Home magazine. She'd done a spread on their owner's house when he'd bought it, and after Blaine explained his situation, Ron had called in a favor. Blaine just hoped this cabin would be enough.

"Thanks for inviting me. You said you'd make it worth my while." Diane's no-nonsense attitude oozed with every fiber of her being. From her pulled back hair to the pressed suit she wore to the three-inch heels gracing her feet that looked like they could double as a weapon in a pinch. Suddenly he wasn't sure she would find this so impressive.

"I hope you'll find this worth a spread in your magazine." He stepped back and allowed her entrance to the cabin. "This cabin has been in my family for years. I inherited it this summer but had no idea what to do with it. I have some before pictures I can show you."

"I've seen them," she said with a wave of her hand as she stepped in, her eyes combing over the living room. She nodded as she walked the floor. "It's definitely nice. Who's the designer?"

Blaine felt his lips twitching. He'd known Kenzi was talented. "A new designer, and one who could really use the exposure. Is it good enough?"

Diane pinched her tight lips together and paused in front of the fireplace. "What's this?" She pointed at the picture of him and Kevin.

Blaine paused, but he didn't feel the suffocating pressure he usually felt. "That's a picture of my brother and me. We used to come here every summer as a family. I hired Kenzi to redo the cabin because I was planning to sell it."

"Why?" Diane turned to him with a quizzical expression. "It's such a beautiful space and location."

"Because Kevin died here. In the lake out back."

Her eyes widened, and her mouth fell open in shock.

"But Kenzi showed me there was still life here. She added that picture to remind me of the good times we had. To help me forget about the bad. She's not just a designer. She's a healer as well." He hadn't meant to tell the story of his brother, and he hadn't planned to talk about Kenzi, but even as the words spilled out, he knew they were the truth. Kenzi had healed him in more ways than one.

Diane turned back to the picture and stared at it again. "I think this is a piece our readers will love." When she faced him again, her stern features were gone, replaced by a sincere smile. "And whoever this Kenzi is, I hope you've scooped her up before some other man does."

Blaine returned the grin. "I'm working on it, and this will definitely help."

"Good. I'll be back with my camera."

KENZI

Kenzi stared at the woman's name on the slip of paper and bit her nail. She wanted to reach out, to do something for Blaine, but what if this was overstepping? He'd made such strides since the first outing with Darby. She could see his heart opening up every time she was around him, but now Christmas was quickly approaching, and she had yet to hear him discuss plans of seeing his family. She knew he was slowly healing the part of his heart that had died with Kevin, but could she help him heal his family as well?

Taking a deep breath, she picked up her cell phone and dialed the number. She'd managed to get his mother's name from him during their conversations and then she'd spent an hour scouring the internet for the woman's number. Lisa Hollis had turned out to be a fairly common name, but after calling the first nine numbers on the list, she was sure this one would be his mother.

"Hello? This is Lisa."

The woman's voice was nothing like she had expected. Though she'd never met the woman, she'd created a picture in her head from Blaine's description. Haggard was the best word that came to mind. A woman beaten down from losing her youngest son and her husband in one year then being forced to work two jobs to provide for the oldest son she rarely saw, but the voice on the other end of the phone was light, sweet.

"Um, hello, my name is Kenzi Lanham. You don't know me, but I was wondering if you are Blaine Hollis's mother." Kenzi bit her lip as she waited for the woman's response. She'd practiced what she was going to say over and over before she'd called, but she still wondered if it was too forceful, too bold.

The silence stretched so long that Kenzi feared the woman had hung up, but finally she spoke. "Yes, my son's name is Blaine. What is this about?"

Kenzi sighed with relief and sent a prayer up both thanking God and asking for the right words. "I'm his girlfriend, and I was hoping that maybe you could help me bring a little Christmas magic to him this year."

"What did you have in mind?" the woman asked.

There was still a hint of hesitation in her voice, but Kenzi could make out the curiosity as well.

"Well, I'm not sure if you know but Blaine volunteers occasionally at a local center here in Southlake. Every year we have a Christmas party for the children. This year we're hosting it a little before Christmas since the Tornadoes play on Christmas Eve. Blaine will be there reading to the children, and I was hoping you could come by."

Another long bout of silence followed before the woman spoke. "Blaine is working with kids?"

Kenzi couldn't help but smile on the other end. It had obviously been awhile since Blaine and his mother had connected. "He is. In fact, he even took on a "little sister" with the program and plans to take her fishing next summer. I think you'll find Blaine a slightly different person from the last time you saw him. So, will you come?"

"I wouldn't miss it for the world," the woman said.

"Great." Kenzi rattled off the details and ended the call. One down and one to go.

"Oh, thank goodness, Blaine, can you help me hang the tinsel?" Kenzi greeted him with a quick kiss on the cheek before grabbing his hand and pulling him across the gym floor.

"Uh, sure." He tightened his hold on the package in his arms as he followed her. He supposed it would have to wait until he could steal her attention for a minute.

She stopped at the far end of the wall where a chair, doubling as a ladder, sat. "Can you hand the tinsel up to me, so I can hang it?" She had a tape dispenser on her wrist and was already pulling out a piece.

Grabbing the tinsel from the floor, he handed it up to her. "Are you sure you don't want me to do that? I am a little taller."

She smiled down at him. "No thanks, I've got it." She

stretched up on her tiptoes and just managed to attach the tinsel to the wall before losing her footing and tumbling off the chair.

Blaine dropped the package in his hands, thankful it wasn't breakable, and caught her just before she hit the floor.

She splayed her hands across his chest as she tried to regain her footing. A soft pink blush of embarrassment covered her cheeks. "Okay, maybe I didn't have it, but at least I had you to catch me."

His heartbeat increased in his chest as she gazed up at him adoringly. He had definitely fallen for this woman; he could feel it in every fiber of his body. "You'll always have me to catch you, Kenzi. I love you," he whispered before lowering his mouth to hers.

He opened his eyes and blinked at her in surprise when he felt her fingers on his lips instead of her mouth.

"You cannot just tell a girl you love her without giving her time to say it back," she said with a smile. Her hands moved up his chest and to the back of his neck. "I love you too, Blaine Hollis."

He chuckled as he resumed his position and met her lips. Their bodies pressed closer together, and he marveled at how well she fit him.

"Um, not to interrupt, but the kids will be here soon." Shelby's voice interrupted their intimate moment, and they jumped apart.

Blaine ran a hand across his chin as he swallowed first his disappointment and then his chagrin. "Sorry, you're right. What else do you need help with, Kenzi?"

She placed her hands on her hips as she turned and surveyed the room. "Actually, I think we're good."

"Then, can I steal you for a moment?" Blaine asked as he retrieved the package from the floor. He turned his attention to Shelby. "Is there enough time for that?"

She didn't know what was in the package; he hadn't told anyone, but she nodded and smiled. "I think there's enough time for that." She flashed a wink at Kenzi before returning to the office.

"What is this?" Kenzi asked when they were alone again.

"An early Christmas present. I just got it this morning, and it couldn't wait for Christmas Day." He held the thin present out to her.

She took it, her brow furrowing in curiosity. "It feels like a book," she said as her fingers explored the package, "but a very bendy one."

Was she always this slow and meticulous with gifts? He had always been the type to rip it open in eagerness. "Just open it."

She pulled back the paper and stared down at the magazine in confusion. "Novel home? I don't understand. I'm not looking for a new home, nor could I probably afford any in here."

"Will you open it to page seven please?" The excitement bubbling inside of him threatened to spill out and open the magazine for her.

She flipped to the page, eyes widening as she realized what the pictures were. "Is this?"

"My cabin? Yes, and the story is about you and how you not only managed to bring it to life but to convince me to keep it."

Her eyes glistened as they met his. "You're going to keep it?"

"I am. There are some bad memories there, but I had always hoped to make memories with my own family there one day, and the only way to do that is to keep it."

"Blaine, I'm so glad. I think you would have regretted selling it." She looked as if she were going to say more, but the ringing of her phone interrupted her. "Hold on," she said, holding a finger up to Blaine. "This is Kenzi Lanham."

He watched as she listened to the caller on the other end. She blinked as a look of shock covered her face.

"Yes, I'm the designer who did Mr. Hollis's cabin."

He bit back his smile as she paused to listen some more.

"Of course, I would be delighted to take a look at your project. Tomorrow? Yes, I can meet you at four. Thank you."

She ended the call and stared up at him. "I just got a potential job offer."

His smile broke free as he squeezed her arm. "I have a feeling you'll have many more in the future."

"I… I don't know what to say. Thank you."

"No, Kenzi. It's me who owes you thanks. You brought me back to life and helped me heal. I can never repay you for that."

KENZI

Kenzi smiled as she watched Blaine read to the kids. He appeared so relaxed and natural; it was hard to believe he had once been afraid to spend time alone with them. Though they hadn't discussed their future, she could imagine being married to him and watching him read like this to their own kids.

"How did you manage this?"

Kenzi turned to smile at the man and woman next to her. Life had been hard on them both as evidenced by her graying hair and crow's feet and his lack of hair and wrinkles, but her eyes were the same color as Blaine's and his smile was just as bright.

"It wasn't all me. God had a big hand in helping him come around."

Blaine finished his story and set the book down. He

began making his way toward Kenzi, his eyes widening as he spied the woman next to her. "Mom? Dad?"

"Hi, Blaine." Lisa's voice had taken on a more reserved tone, and Kenzi saw her posture tense as she waited to see if Blaine would accept her or not. Joe, his father, stood still as well.

He glanced at Kenzi as he pulled his mother in for a hug before turning to his father and embracing him as well. She saw the silent question in his eyes and smiled. They could share the details later. For now, she was just glad to be sharing this scene with him.

At the buzzing of her phone in her pocket, she excused herself.

"This is Kenzi Lanham," she said when she was far enough out of earshot not to bother anyone with her conversation.

"Kenzi Lanham. This is Mayor Shelley. I have a beach house that I would love to update. I saw your work in Novel Homes today, and I'd like to schedule a meeting with you."

Kenzi's knees nearly buckled beneath her. This was the second call she'd received from the spread in the magazine, and while these interest calls didn't guarantee she would land the job, it was certainly more than she'd had going for her a week ago. She couldn't believe Blaine had done this for her. He had made not only her Christmas wish but all her dreams come true.

Kenzi stepped into her soft pink satin gown and turned so Whitley could zip it up. Then she returned the favor. Shelby had opted for a smaller wedding, so she and Whitley, Tucker's sister, were the only bridesmaids, but that was fine with Kenzi. She'd had her hands full decorating for the wedding, and she was glad the room now was quiet and comfortable and not buzzing with conversation.

She couldn't believe Shelby's wedding day was finally here. Ever since the Christmas party, her life had been a whirlwind of activity. She'd had meetings with potential clients, Shelby's wedding to help plan and decorate, and football games to attend with Blaine. It barely left any time for her and Blaine to just hang out, but she knew that after this wedding was over, at least some of her burden would be lifted.

"That dress is beautiful on you," Shelby said as she adjusted her veil in the mirror. "Both of you."

"Thank you, but I think all eyes will be on the bride. As they should be." Kenzi stepped behind Shelby and leaned down to hug her. She knew she wasn't losing her best friend, but she also knew that marriage changed things. Showing up on her doorstep would be more of an inconvenience and girl's nights out might be harder to come by. Still, she wouldn't change a thing. Shelby was happier than she had ever seen her, and marrying Tucker would only increase that happiness. "You ready?"

"I think so. I'm still trying to adjust to the fact that in an hour my new last name will be Jackson. Shelby Jackson. It still sounds foreign in my mouth."

Whitley laughed and helped Shelby to her feet. "You'll get used to it. Besides, it will make us real sisters."

The two girls hugged, and Kenzi couldn't help feeling just a little jealous. Shelby had two sisters now through marriage, but Kenzi would never have that. Blaine was now an only child, just as she was. There would be no sisters in her future if she married him. Married him? She was getting ahead of herself. They'd been dating for a few months, but he'd offered no hints that a proposal was near.

She grabbed Shelby's bridal bouquet from the table a

few feet away and handed it to her. "I think the new name sounds perfect, and you will get used to it." Then she picked up the two smaller bouquets of pink and white flowers and handed one to Whitley, keeping the other for herself. "Now, let's go get you married."

BLAINE

Blaine couldn't help the smile that spread across his face as he watched Kenzi walk down the aisle. Her eyes stayed locked on his with every step, and he forced himself not to pull out the box that was in his pocket and propose to her right then and there. This was Tucker's day, and he wouldn't ruin that, but he couldn't wait to ask her to be his forever.

She took her place on the other side of the stage. The distance seemed so far. Farther than he wanted to be from her. The music changed, and it took all his effort to turn and face the entrance of the church.

Shelby was a vision in her white dress, and Blaine was elated for his friend, but all he could think about was what Kenzi would look like when it was their turn. Would she want a big wedding? Or something smaller like this?

He thought back to the first day of training camp when Tucker had rattled off all the monotonous details of wedding planning, and he realized as much as he would have hated it then, he would cherish every moment of it now.

The pastor began speaking, but Blaine heard few of the words until he was asked to produce the rings. He'd been floored and honored when Tucker asked him to be his best man, but he'd accepted knowing he might be returning the favor before too much longer.

Tucker and Shelby exchanged their vows, kissed, and then the wedding was over. He held out his arm for Kenzi and followed the bride and groom out of the sanctuary and toward the reception area. The box burned in his pocket, but the time wasn't right yet. Just a little longer.

He tried to focus on the food and the toast during the reception, but it was no use.

"What is going on with you?" Kenzi asked as he led her to the dance floor when it was time.

"Nothing. I'm just enjoying the moment and how beautiful you look."

Kenzi furrowed her brow at him but stepped into his arms. "You look pretty dapper yourself."

"Good, I would hate to look scruffy on the day I ask you to be my wife." He twirled her around and waited for the words to sink in.

"The day you do what?" she asked when she was facing him again.

He stopped moving and dropped to his knee. Around them, the crowd stilled and every eye in the place turned to them. He hoped Tucker wouldn't mind the minor interruption as he reached into his pocket and pulled out the black box.

"Kenzi Lanham, you have changed my life and made it worth living again. I would be a fool to ever let you go. I love you, and while I know I'm not the man you deserve yet, I promise to get better every day. Will you marry me?"

A single tear escaped out of the corner of Kenzi's eye before she nodded and held out her hand. The crowd around them cheered as he placed the diamond ring on her finger and rose to kiss her.

"Just so you know," she whispered as she pulled back. "You are the perfect man, and I'm the one who would be a fool to let you go. I love you Blaine."

As he picked her up and twirled her around, he knew this was just the beginning, and though he couldn't see him, somehow, he knew Kevin was smiling down on him.

THE END!

IF YOU LOVED BLAINE AND SHELBY'S STORY, THEN YOU won't want to miss Mason's story. Be sure to preorder your copy of Touchdown on Love today!

. . .

AND IF YOU ENJOYED THIS STORY, PLEASE LEAVE A REVIEW. Reviews help other readers find books they will enjoy.

❧ 21 ❧
NOT READY TO SAY GOODBYE YET?

LOVE ON THE LINE IS THE SECOND BOOK IN THE TEXAS Tornado series. Continue the journey with Touchdown on Love — Mason's story

Touchdown on Love

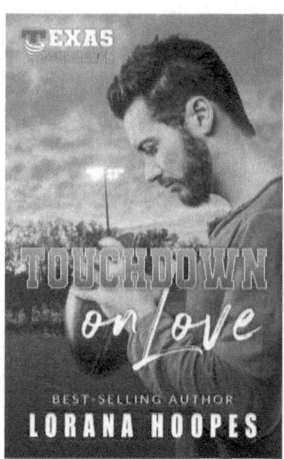

He's the wide receiver who had his heart broken.

She's the new team doctor.

When the present throws them back together, will they find their way back to their past

CLICK HERE TO PREORDER TOUCHDOWN ON LOVE AND turn the page for a special sneak peek.

❧ 22 ❧

SNEAK PEEK AT TOUCHDOWN
ON LOVE

Coming soon!
Click here to preorder Touchdown on Love.
Releasing soon!

23

A FREE STORY FOR YOU

Enjoyed this story? Not ready to quit reading yet? If you sign up for my newsletter, you will receive The Billionaire's Impromptu Bet right away as my thank you gift for choosing to hang out with me.

The Billionaire's Impromptu Bet

A SWAT officer. A bored billionaire heiress. A bet that could change everything….

Read on for a taste of The Billionaire's Impromptu Bet….

24

THE BILLIONAIRE'S IMPROMPTU
BET PREVIEW

Brie Carter fell back spread eagle on her queen-sized canopy bed sending her blonde hair fanning out behind her. With a large sigh, she uttered, "I'm bored."

"How can you be bored? You have like millions of dollars." Her friend, Ariel, plopped down in a seated position on the bed beside her and flicked her raven hair off her shoulder. "You want to go shopping? I hear Tiffany's is having a special right now."

Brie rolled her eyes. Shopping? Where was the excitement in that? With her three platinum cards, she could go shopping whenever she wanted. "No, I'm bored with shopping too. I have everything. I want to do something exciting. Something we don't normally do."

Brie enjoyed being rich. She loved the unlimited credit

cards at her disposal, the constant apparel of new clothes, and of course the penthouse apartment her father paid for, but lately, she longed for something more fulfilling.

Ariel's hazel eyes widened. "I know. There's a new bar down on Franklin Street. Why don't we go play a little game?"

Brie sat up, intrigued at the secrecy and the twinkle in Ariel's eyes. "What kind of game?"

"A betting game. You let me pick out any man in the place. Then you try to get him to propose to you."

Brie wrinkled her nose. "But I don't want to get married." She loved her freedom and didn't want to share her penthouse with anyone, especially some man.

"You don't marry him, silly. You just get him to propose."

Brie bit her lip as she thought. It had been awhile since her last relationship and having a man dote on her for a month might be interesting, but…. "I don't know. It doesn't seem very nice."

"How about I sweeten the pot? If you win, I'll set you up on a date with my brother."

Brie cocked her head. Was she serious? The only thing Brie couldn't seem to buy in the world was the affection of Ariel's very handsome, very wealthy, brother. He was a movie star, just the kind of person Brie could consider marrying in the future. She'd had a crush on him as long as she and Ariel had been friends, but he'd always seen her as just that, his little sister's friend. "I thought you didn't want me dating your brother."

"I don't." Ariel shrugged. "But he's between girl-friends right now, and I know you've wanted it for ages. If you win this bet, I'll set you up. I can't guarantee any more than one date though. The rest will be up to you."

Brie wasn't worried about that. Charm she possessed in abundance. She simply needed some alone time with him, and she was certain she'd be able to convince him they were meant to be together. "All right. You've got a deal."

Ariel smiled. "Perfect. Let's get you changed then and see who the lucky man will be.

A tiny tug pulled on Brie's heart that this still wasn't right, but she dismissed it. This was simply a means to an end, and he'd never have to know.

JESSE CALHOUN RELAXED AS THE RHYTHMIC THUDDING OF the speed bag reached his ears. Though he loved his job, it was stressful being the SWAT sniper. He hated having to take human lives and today had been especially rough. The team had been called out to a drug bust, and Jesse was forced to return fire at three hostiles. He didn't care that they fired at his team and himself first. Taking a life was always hard, and every one of them haunted his dreams.

"You gonna bust that one too?" His co-worker Brendan

appeared by his side. Brendan was the opposite of Jesse in nearly every way. Where Jesse's hair was a dark copper, Brendan's was nearly black. Jesse sported paler skin and a dusting of freckles across his nose, but Brendan's skin was naturally dark and freckle free.

Jesse flashed a crooked grin, but kept his eyes on the small, swinging black bag. The speed bag was his way to release, but a few times he had started hitting while still too keyed up and he had ruptured the bag. Okay, five times, but who was counting really? Besides, it was a better way to calm his nerves than other things he could choose. Drinking, fights, gambling, women.

"Nah, I think this one will last a little longer." His shoulders began to burn, and he gave the bag another few punches for good measure before dropping his arms and letting it swing to a stop. "See? It lives to be hit at least another day." Every once in a while, Jesse missed training the way he used to. Before he joined the force, he had been an amateur boxer, on his way to being a pro, but a shoulder injury had delayed his training and forced him to consider something else. It had eventually healed, but by then he had lost his edge.

"Hey, why don't you come drink with us?" Brendan clapped a hand on Jesse's shoulder as they headed into the locker room.

"You know I don't drink." Jesse often felt like the outsider of the team. While half of the six-man team was married, the other half found solace in empty bottles and meaningless relationships. Jesse understood that — their job was such that they never knew if they would come home night after night — but he still couldn't partake.

Brendan opened his locker and pulled out a clean shirt. He peeled off his current one and added deodorant before tugging on the new one. "You don't have to drink. Look, I won't drink either. Just come and hang out with us. You have no one waiting for you at home."

That wasn't entirely true. Jesse had Bugsy, his Boston Terrier, but he understood Brendan's point. Most days, Jesse went home, fed Bugsy, made dinner, and fell asleep watching TV on the couch. It wasn't much of a life. "All right, I'll go, but I'm not drinking."

Brendan's lips pulled back to reveal his perfectly white teeth. He bragged about them, but Jesse knew they were veneers. "That's the spirit. Hurry up and change. We don't want to leave the rest of the team waiting."

"Is everyone coming?" Jesse pulled out his shower necessities. Brendan might feel comfortable going out with just a new application of deodorant, but Jesse needed to wash more than just dirt and sweat off. He needed to wash the sound of the bullets and the sight of lifeless bodies from his mind.

"Yeah, Pat's wife is pregnant again and demanding some crazy food concoctions. Pat agreed to pick them up if she let him have an hour. Cam and Jared's wives are having a girls' night, so the whole gang can be together. It will be nice to hang out when we aren't worried about being shot at."

"Fine. Give me ten minutes. Unlike you, I like to clean up before I go out."

Brendan smirked. "I've never had any complaints. Besides, do you know how long it takes me to get my hair like this?"

Jesse shook his head as he walked into the shower, but he knew it was true. Brendan had rugged good looks and muscles to match. He rarely had a hard time finding a woman. Jesse on the other hand hadn't dated anyone in the last few months. It wasn't that he hadn't been looking, but he was quieter than his teammates. And he wasn't looking for right now. He was looking for forever. He just hadn't found it yet.

Click here to continue reading The Billionaire's Impromptu Bet.

THE STORY DOESN'T END!

You've met a few people and fallen in love....

I bet you're wondering how you can meet everyone else.

Star Lake Series:

When Love Returns: Can Presley and Brandon forget past hurts or will their stubborn natures keep them apart forever?

Once Upon a Star: Now that Blake has gained confidence and some muscle, will he finally be able to reveal his feelings to Audrey?

Love Conquers All: Now that Azarius has another chance with Laney, will he find the courage to share his life with her? Or will his emotional walls create a barrier that will leave him alone once more?

The Heartbeats Series:

Where It All Began: Will Sandra tell Henry her darkest secret? And will she ever be able to forgive herself and find healing? Find out in this emotional love story.

The Power of Prayer: Who will Callie choose and how will her choice affect the rest of her life? Find out in this touching novel.

When Hearts Collide: Amanda captivates his heart, but can Jared save her from making the biggest mistake of her life? A must read for mothers and daughters.

A Past Forgiven: Can Chad leave his bad-boy image behind and step up and be there for Jess and the baby?

Sweet Billionaires Series:

The Billionaire's Secret: Can Max really change his philandering ways? Or will one mistake seal his fate forever?

A Brush with a Billionaire: Will Brent and Sam's stubborn natures keep them apart or can a small town festival bring them together?

The Billionaire's Christmas Miracle: Drew Devonshire is captivated by the woman he meets at a masquerade ball, but who is she?

The Billionaire's Cowboy Groom: When Carrie returns to town requesting a divorce, can he convince her they belong together?

The Cowboy Billionaire: Coming Soon!

The Lawkeeper Series:

Lawfully Matched: Will Jesse find his fiancee's

killer? And when Kate flies into his life, will he be able to put his painful past behind him in order to love again?

Lawfully Justified: Can Emma offer William a reason to stay? Can William find a way to heal from his broken past to start a future with Emma? Or will a haunting secret take away all the possibilities of this budding romance?

The Scarlet Wedding: William and Emma are planning their wedding, but an outbreak and a return from his past force them to change their plans. Is a happily ever after still in their future?

Lawfully Redeemed: Dani Higgins is a K9 cop looking to make a name for herself, but she finds herself at the mercy of a stranger after an accident. Calvin Phillips just wanted to help his brother, but somehow he ended up in the middle of a police investigation and caring for the woman trying to bring his brother in.

The Still Small Voice Series:

The Still Small Voice: Will Kat be able to give up control and do what God is asking of her?

A Spark in the Darkness coming soon!

Blushing Brides Series:

The Cowboy's Reality Bride: Laney Swann has been running from her past for years, but it takes meeting a man on a reality dating show to make her see there's no need to run.

The Reality Bride's Baby: Laney wants nothing more

than a baby, but when she starts feeling dizzy is it pregnancy or something more serious?

The Producer's Unlikely Bride: Ava McDermott is waiting for the perfect love, but after agreeing to a fake relationship with Justin, she finds herself falling for real.

Ava's Blessing in Disguise: Five years after marriage, Ava faces a mysterious illness that threatens to ruin her career. Will she find out what it is?

The Soldier's Steadfast Bride: coming soon

The Men of Fire Beach

Fire Games: Cassidy returns home from Who Wants to Marry a Cowboy to find obsessive letters from a fan. The cop assigned to help her wants to get back to his case, but what she sees at a fire may just be the key he's looking for.

Lost Memories and New Beginnings: She has no idea who she is. He's the doctor caring for her. When her past collides with his present, can he keep her safe?

When Questions Abound A companion story to Lost Memories, this book tells the story from Detective Jordan Graves's point of view.

Never Forget the Past

Secrets and Suspense coming soon!

Stand Alones:

Love Renewed: This books is part of the multi author second chance series. When fate reunites high school sweethearts separated by life's choices, can they find a second chance at love at a snowy lodge amid a little mystery?

Her children's early reader chapter book series:
The Wishing Stone #1: Dangerous Dinosaur
The Wishing Stone #2: Dragon Dilemma
The Wishing Stone #3: Mesmerizing Mermaids
The Wishing Stone #4: Pyramid Puzzle
The Wishing Stone Inspirations 1: Mary's Miracle
To see a list of all her books

authorloranahoopes.com
loranahoopes@gmail.com

DISCUSSION QUESTIONS

1. What was your favorite scene in the book? What made it your favorite?

2. Did you have a favorite line in the book? What do you think made it so memorable?

3. Who was your favorite character in the book and why?

4. Blaine faced issues of self- blame in the book. Do you think they were justified?

5. What do you think would be the hardest part about dating a celebrity?

6. What did you learn about God from reading this book?

7. How can you use that knowledge in your life from now on?

8. What can you take away from Blaine and Kenzi's relationship?

9. What do you think would make the story even better?